LONG DIVISION: STORIES OF SOCIAL DECAY, SOCIETAL COLLAPSE, AND BAD MANNERS
Copyright © 2024 by Bad Hand Books
Print ISBN: 979-8-9881286-7-0

Anthology edited by Doug Murano ÷ Michael Bailey
Cover artwork by J.E. Larson
Interior ÷ cover design by Michael Bailey | Written Backwards

Bad Hand Books
www.badhandbooks.com

# LONG DIVISION

## STORIES OF SOCIAL DECAY, SOCIETAL COLLAPSE AND BAD MANNERS

÷

EDITED BY
DOUG MURANO ÷ MICHAEL BAILEY

# CONTENTS

# CONTENTS

# LONG DIVISION

# ZOJE STAGE

## THE MEAN SEASON

÷

The Mean Season: a new era when reason
is abandoned and all souls battle—
with words, with forks—
for a scrap of victory.

A plague unlike a flu—it flows endless,
bottomless, carrying everything we once
knew of ourselves
away.

I woke up one morning with the urge to kill—
a quite separate feeling from the previous thrill
of grinding my neighbors beneath my feet,
gleeful as their dignity—red, full, and complete—
bled into the gutter.

One by one we are let loose from the constraints—
which once dictated the manner of most common
complaints—
set free to see, speak, squawk and simmer
over trespasses and slights, as urges quite dimmer
make savages of us all.

It appears one day
like a blinded dog in need of food

The first reaction "Who did this?"
quickly becomes "I will feed you"
and then "I will make you mine."

It appears one day
like a tooth on a pillow

The first reaction "What is this?"
quickly becomes "It is a gift"
and then "With this I shall devour you."

It appears one day
like a flower with thorns

The first reaction "It hurts"
quickly becomes "It is beautiful"
and then "I will share it with everyone."

# ALEX GRECIAN

## ITEM G2V

÷

BIDDING is set to begin at noon, but time is elastic and the auctioneer has decided he will start when he's ready. The bidders sit on folding chairs; thirty rows of twenty chairs. Heads of state are seated next to CEOs and tech pioneers; recluses and movie stars and criminals sit side by side, while journalists, scientists, and politicians line the walls, standing, leaning, jockeying amongst themselves for better positions. The aisles have been cleared, and the doors have been locked, but there's a video camera mounted to the ceiling and there are monitors in the streets outside where crowds have gathered, many hoping a door will open so they can slip inside. People around the world are hunched in front of their computers or over their phones, watching the live feed. Every television channel is broadcasting the event. Commentators bicker about the significance of the auction, and debate its repercussions. One channel is hosting a roundtable discussion of auction-deniers, each of whom has a different take on why the auction can't really be happening. Even so, it's the most important day any of them can remember.

As if there are days.

*The biggest manufacturer of solar panels in China has declared bankruptcy. So have its competitors. Wind, however, remains a viable energy source, and the changing tides have led to an increased*

*interest in water energy. The consumer run on fluorescent lightbulbs has created a temporary global shortage.*

A low murmur is heard throughout the room as Item G2V is wheeled across the stage on a stand. The item is roughly the size of a silver dollar. It is displayed under a tinted dome. Everyone in the room is wearing dark glasses, but several in the front row shield their eyes with their hands. No one looks directly at Item G2V.

The auctioneer clears his throat and looks at his notes. He is a former secretary-general of the United Nations. He moves his gavel, aligning it with the edge of the podium, and glances at the back of the room where the consignor stands watching. He is wearing what he always wears: a floppy straw hat, jorts, and a tank top with a faded rainbow across the chest. The strap of one of his sandals has been broken and repaired, and it appears ready to break again. After the auction he'll be able to buy a million new pairs of sandals, a billion, but he won't. He doesn't care about the money. He hopes his hobby will be taken seriously after this. He's already received speaking invitations from universities and scientific institutions. He thinks a rising tide carries all ships. He thinks he and his fellow collectors will now be respected. He can't believe he started this only two weeks ago.

As if there are weeks.

He had followed rumors of a *Mitchell's Satyr* to a field outside Michigan, and had crept around for hours in the tall grass carrying a net, his backpack full of plastic jars and cotton balls and vials of ethyl acetate, but had seen nothing more exotic than a *Cabbage White*.

The sun pressed down on him and squeezed the air from his lungs. It baked the brown grass around him, filling the air with a yellowish odor. His hair under the cap of his straw hat was soaking wet; sweat rolled down his forehead, skipped over his eyebrows and stung his eyes. He swallowed a bug and gagged; he squinted at the washed out, threadbare sky. Dammit, he said. He laid down his pack and stretched out on his back in the stiff grass. He closed his eyes and saw red, saw the capillaries in his eyelids.

And he had an idea.

He rolled onto his side and rummaged through his bag, grabbed a jar and a square of white cardboard. He grinned at his foolishness

and held up the jar. He placed it over the white-yellow disk and slid the cardboard over the opening, and when he lowered it to his lap the world changed.

He reached for a lid.

*Certain species of algae have died, along with the fish and insects that depended on the algae for food. Birds everywhere are quiet, but there has been a gradual increase in the population of bats. Grain is rationed worldwide as farmland is converted to the cultivation of mushrooms.*

The auctioneer checks his pocket watch and begins.

"I don't believe Item G2V needs an explanation," he says. "We all know why we're here and what we're bidding on. We have six hundred interested parties in this room, and many thousands more participating electronically. I would like to offer a word of caution. The winning bidder will gain a great deal of power, of course, but a great burden, as well, and I implore you to act with humanity's best interests at heart. He clears his throat again, and takes a deep breath. Let's get to it, shall we? The opening bid is one million, he says. Do I have one million?

There is laughter, and six hundred paddles are raised at once. A thousand electronic bids are registered, then ten thousand, a hundred thousand, all being checked against accounts and holdings in real time.

A reporter steps forward and raises her hand. She is from The Tamil Mirror in Sri Lanka. Give it back to the people, she says. Put it back where it belongs. There is more laughter, this time slightly uncomfortable. There has been a lot of debate on this subject, and public opinion is on the reporter's side. Eleven countries have signed laws preventing the procurement and sale of Item G2V, but it is generally thought they are trying to lock the barn after the horse has gone. The auction house has verified the provenance of the item, and has declared that the auction shall proceed as scheduled. There is no point in denying the reality of the situation, and besides, there are people more powerful than the reporter who have declared an interest in Item G2V. They will not be denied their chance to bid.

The auctioneer gestures and the woman is ushered from the room. When the door opens there's a push to get in, but United

Nations peacekeepers are there to maintain order. They wear riot gear. The door is closed again and relocked. The auctioneer apologizes for the interruption and raises the bid. Two million. Do I have two?

Six hundred paddles go up. More than three hundred thousand electronic bids are registered.

*Temperatures have plummeted across the globe. Shallow rivers and lakes have frozen over. Fishing boats and ferries are stranded at sea, unable to plow through ice shelves at every port and beach. Glow-in-the-dark winter gear is the biggest fashion trend of the season, and a new FBI division investigates fraudulent sources of vitamin D supplements and frostbite creams.*

A man in a dark suit walks out onto the stage and whispers in the auctioneer's ear. There is muttered speculation in the hall. The auctioneer nods and picks up his gavel and the audience goes quiet again. The man in the dark suit trots back across the stage.

I've been told I'm being too conservative, the auctioneer says. I've been told we don't have all day. I have two million, do I have a billion?

Six hundred paddles go up. A hundred and four electronic bids are registered. Two are stricken for insufficient funds.

I have a billion, do I have ten billion?

Four hundred paddles go up. There are three electronic bids. One is stricken.

I have ten billion, do I have a hundred billion?

Six paddles go up. There is one electronic bid.

The auctioneer takes a breath. Do I have two hundred billion?

One paddle goes up. There is one electronic bid.

I have two hundred billion, do I have three?

There is one electronic bid.

*Mars and Saturn move closer to Jupiter as it becomes the center of the solar system. The Earth begins to orbit Jupiter, too, and its rotation changes, rendering clocks and calendars useless. New words have been invented to describe the passage of time, but none have caught on. Pocket watches are popular novelty gifts.*

A truck rolls up to a small house in Scotland. Three men get out. They are wearing fur-lined parkas and bulletproof vests. One listens to an earpiece and nods. There are twelve snipers stationed at

vantage points around them, rifles trained on every twist in the road below. The road has been cordoned off. There have been several violent attempts to halt the transport of Item G2V. There have been mass protests. The identity of the winning bidder and the delivery route from the auction house are state secrets. The back of the truck opens and the delivery man steps carefully to the ground. He is carrying a wooden crate. The other men from the truck surround him as he walks up the long driveway.

An old man emerges from the house. He is alone. He is the winning bidder. One of the snipers adjusts his position and aims his rifle at the old man. The woman next to him chuckles and shakes her head, and the sniper shrugs. Who would blame me, he says . But he turns and points his rifle at the road again.

The winning bidder takes the crate from the delivery man and tips him two dollars. He returns to the house. The delivery man, a five-star general in the American Army, waits for a minute then walks slowly back down the driveway to the truck that will take him to a waiting helicopter. The snipers stand down. They are among the most decorated military personnel on Earth. Many have never met before. Two will become lifelong friends. Two will kill each other within the month.

As if there are months.

*More than seventeen thousand butterfly species are thought to be extinct in the wild. A common Cabbage White was the last to be spotted. Only the nocturnal Hedylidae has been sighted by collectors. The moth population, meanwhile, flourishes worldwide, and nine new cricket species have been identified.*

The winning bidder has sent his staff home. He is alone in the house. He takes the crate to a marble-topped table in his living room. There is a crowbar on the table, and a hammer. And a welding mask. He pounds an end of the crowbar under the crate's lid and pries it up. He pulls out handfuls of sawdust and drops them on the floor, creating clouds of dust that make him cough. The staff will return in the morning. Someone will clean up the mess. When he sees the glass dome, the old man reaches in and lifts it out, spilling more sawdust on the floor and across the tops of his trainers. He holds up Item G2V and admires it, but does not look directly at it.

He expected it to be heavier.

There is a feeling he sometimes gets when he has beaten someone in a deal or bought something outrageously rare. It is as if he is the most important person in the world. He carries the dome on its steel base through the house and down a dark stairwell to his basement. At the bottom of the stairs is a thick door with a keypad. He enters a password and raises the welding mask, allowing a laser to scan his retinae. The door slides open and he carries his three-hundred- billion-dollar purchase into a room the size of the entire house above. The walls of this room are lined with velvet covered shelves. There are eight glass-topped display cases in the middle of the room. There are motion sensors in the ceiling, and pressure sensors in the floor. The temperature and humidity are controlled by a system of his own design. Every item on the shelves and in the cases is carefully labeled: the fractured skull of a European dictator and the bullet that killed him, the mummified foot of a Tibetan creature that probably never existed, a communication device purported to have belonged to an interstellar scout, stuffed and mounted specimens of several dozen extinct species, and on and on. There is an empty space waiting on a shelf at the back of the room. The old man has already created a label for Item G2V. He positions the glass dome in its place and steps back to admire his acquisition.

*Impressive*, he thinks.

He thinks, *I am an important man.*

*The earth trembles.*

# CHUCK PALAHNIUK

## CELESTE

÷

NOBODY sent a card. Most times when it's a birthday or somebody dies we pass a card around for the crew to sign. The gaffers and lighting techs, they write, "You were a candle in the wind," or, "Sorry to hear you shot yourself." It's just something we do to support the talent.

Even if it's AIDS that eats up a performer—not a happy ending—even while the studio's doing damage control and all the talent is counting backward about who did what with whom going back to the dead girl, and was it unprotected, even then we send a card around for the crew to sign. Maybe we send flowers. Not so much this time on account of, well, the performer being Celeste.

Princess Celeste. Celeste the pest.

Celeste went overboard with the rules. She was always about *No hitting* and *Do NOT slap my face*. And if a performer by accident back-handed her a *blat* across her cheek she'd turn *red*-red and wallop him. That's after the director tells her to cry. A girl crying looks sexy. A girl all red-faced and driving her knee into a naked man with a boner, slam, her knee into the boner ... not so sexy.

Celeste handed down all these silly ultimatums about not pissing in her mouth and *No Human Toilet* and *Don't go while you're inside me* and no big scary-big dildos and especially no glass dildos despite Linda Lovelace doing glass dildos, and no bareback, especially no bareback, and no waxing because a waxed cooch is a breeding ground for MRSA, and no whipped cream because dairy products down there are a sure-fire yeast infection, and one day an AD says to her, "Celeste, nobody hired you for your stupid boundaries."

And the AD said, "Can't you just be your tits for two hours?" And Celeste walked off the set and got the guy's hours cut in half.

She had all these stupid extra rules about no animals and no Rohypnol. No kidding, Celeste, she was about the least creative artist in the business. No even pretend-blatting her across the face to knock the spooge out of her mouth, and it's not even real spooge on account of another rule. It's Elmer's glue shot out of a bottle somebody has to squeeze outside the shot, and even then she clamps her eyes and mouth shut like she's facing a firing squad. Another time, she could've pocketed a quick five hundred bucks. The bit called for her to poo on top of a glass coffee table while a performer lay under it and spooged. Easy money.

Celeste had asked for a bathroom break anyway, but right then the Lady Celeste gets up on her high horse and invents some new cack-assed rule about *No pooing on glass coffee tables with a guy underneath.* And she went to the toilet and just threw away five hundred bucks. And another time she's limping round half a day when a performer went a hair off-center and nailed her in the muscle instead of the middle, and there's nobody in this business who hasn't been nailed by a foul ball to the cherry blossom, and after that she says no going in her hair. And no clothespins. And *Douching for anal messes with my gut flora.*

And by now you should be thinking *What a fucking, stuck-up snowflake!*

Celeste the pest gets the production company on the ropes. Then out of nowhere she skinnies down. She really skinnies down, the wrong kind of skinny, so we give Celeste her walking papers, and it's so long, Princess. So skinny she can't even do OnlyFans.

We have a business to run. This isn't a damn hospice.

It's after that we don't bother to send a card or flowers. That's after we cut the price on the girl's backlist titles. Nothing moves the dusty units faster than a girl dying.

And it's right here you should be thinking *Boo-hoo! What comes around, goes around, bitch!*

It's after that we're shooting this orgy. We're talking about a lot of moving parts. The blocking is like some old English recipe where you stick a pigeon inside of a chicken inside a rabbit inside a goose inside a pig inside a cow and cook it so nobody can guess what meat they're eating. We're cutting the dailies, trying to match up head shots and meat shots, and in the background behind the missionary and just off the doggy-style stands this shape. It's nobody. Not a gaffer, it's just this shape looking dead-center into the lens of Camera One, but what's messed up is when we cut to Camera Two and Camera Three those eyes are staring straight into them as well.

No matter how gifted they are, no talent can look into three cameras at the same time, but this standing-there shape, you can see a picture on the wall. Right through this figure, we can see the picture, and then a performer spooges and the spooge flies right through this apparition and splashes a ceramic panther.

A whole day's work, and we've got jack shit we can use. The next day, same deal. A little clearer this time, a little more in focus, but the figure is glaring into every camera, wrecking every shot. What gives it away is the figure's skin. Big red lesions eat up the skin, classic Rock Hudson craters and blood blisters all over the arms and legs so skinny the elbows and knees look like big knots tied in a rope. A thin rope. And on one arm, tattooed down one skinny forearm are the scrolly words "No Glove, No Love." And that gives it away.

It's Princess Don't-Spit-In-My-Mouth. It's Lady Only-Water-Based-Lubricants-Please!

And what you need to wrap your head around is we're the fifth-largest creator of adult content in northwestern, south-central rural Indiana, and we have subscribers to answer to. If we don't post fresh product to our site every week, don't count on brand loyalty. Our customer base wants to put mileage on their greasy hands every day.

We go on location to shoot at the Comfort Inn, and Celeste shows up to stare at us as if it's our fault she's an eaten-up AIDS monster with boney bird-girl claws and a mouthful of cottage-cheesy thrush infection.

The studio is drowning in red ink, and by now you should be thinking *Celeste is a really poor sport!*

The higher-ups headhunt some crystal guru who smudges up the studio with burning sage. The guru boils bay leaves and lemons, and sprinkles salt water, and we shoot a quick girl-girl test, and Celeste stands right there, and nobody wants dead-girl ghosts in their porn, especially not the Japanese market. No, the Japanese can jerk to anything except a dead, rotten AIDS girl staring at them with scary, stringy hair hanging down. So the higher-ups consult with a priest, not just a performer wearing a collar who flops his huge wanger through the window during Confession, but a real Roman Catholic Father wearing pants and probably underwear. As a test, this priest asks us to shoot a quick boy-boy, and there's Celeste all rotted out with AIDS patches and syphilis where her nose should be and her eyes the color of hepatitis, dead Celeste upstaging and photobombing the hot father-on-stepson action, so the priest throws holy water around, and little good that does us.

Between the spooge and salt water and holy water, the set, let's say the flats and the leather sofa have seen better days.

Here the higher-ups bring in an egghead from some college who asks for a sit-down, alone with Celeste. A para-psychiatrist. So we clear the set and leave the camera to run on this professor while we all sit outside in our cars, and later on the tape the professor is saying, "I understand, Celeste," and, "That sounds perfectly reasonable." Celeste, all boney and running with sores, she stands, not saying anything, but the professor says, "We'll make that happen."

The professor gives us the name of Celeste's mom so we can fly her in. No MILF, she is, the mom. From the look of her, she has maybe one egg left, but the professor says to pair her with our lead male performer and poke a hole in the rubber. Celeste's mother asks what's this all about? She says her daughter is a stenographer and they're estranged, so we give her just a hint of Rohypnol, just a drop in her cappuccino, and shoot the scene, and the moment the performer spooges inside Celeste's mom, the rotting, dead AIDS ghost, she disappears. *Poof!*

After that, we're back in business. No ghost. Celeste gets another

shot at life, and maybe this time she'll get it right and become a court stenographer. Her mom is her mom yet again.

That's until Randy Morningwood shoots himself. He eats a pistol, after we had to lay him off, and it's not like we need another washed-up, has-been staring back at us from the dead.

So the higher-ups scramble to get a sympathy card, a big card, and to order flowers for the funeral. A ton of flowers. The crew writes nice stuff in the card this time. We cut the price on all the old Morningwood videos, and the units start to fly off the shelves, and that's about as happy an ending as we're probably going to get.

# ANNA TABORSKA

## THIRD-TIME LUCY

÷

LUCY lay on the bare mattress, staring into the corner of the ceiling directly above her. She could no longer see the web there or the spider that had woven it. The large house spider had worked for hours, secreting silk from her spinnerets and arranging the threads into a sturdy and intricate lair. But Lucy's failing eyesight had registered little more than the occasional movement as the spider emerged to survey her web or despatch her infrequent prey.

Like many of the residents of the doomed South Acton Estate, Lucy was succumbing to the group punishment meted out for non-payment of the Window Tax: the boarding up of windows in buildings whose residents were unable to pay the extortionate levy imposed on each of them for every single pane of glass in their own flat and in all the communal areas combined. Lucy had only lived on the Estate for seven years—since AI had taken over her industry and she had become, quite literally, redundant—but some of her neighbours, who'd lived in the dark for generations, were now completely blind, and a woman down the hall had even given birth to a little girl with no eyes at all.

Poverty and the intense heat outside the vast concrete buildings that made up the Estate kept the residents inside their small, dark apartments, lying down much of the time to conserve what little energy the constant hunger had not yet robbed them of. The Estate had once boasted colourful allotments, with a separate small garden assigned to each flat, where the residents could grow their own fruit and veg, and rest in the shade of the London plane trees that grew nearby. But the introduction of water rationing led to the imposing of heavy fines on those who tried to keep their gardens alive, and the Government used the subsequent so-called Allotment Riots as an excuse to sell off the green space of the South Acton Estate to a major development corporation, which turned the land into the luxurious Southfield Shopping Centre, combined with top-end housing for the super-rich. A vast wall was erected between the dingy tower blocks of the South Acton Estate and the posh Southfield complex: a living green wall of automatically-watered vertically-bedded plants and flowers on the Southfield side and, on the South Acton Estate side, a wall covered in anti-climb paint and crowned with razor wire.

÷

LUCY wasn't sure if it was day or night. Not that it really mattered. These days, she slept as much as she could; sleeping kept the hunger at bay, as well as the pain in the stump of what had once been her left arm. And the dull ache in the stump wasn't the worst of it. Much harder to bear was the excruciating pain in the arm that was no longer there. *Phantom pain*, the doctor had called it. Pain for which there was no remedy; pain that was sometimes replaced by an unscratchable itch that drove Lucy insane for hours at a time. If only she could fall asleep, it would all go away for a little while.

Lucy closed her eyes and tried to picture herself lying in a lush meadow, full of flowers and butterflies. She never could understand why someone had named them *butterflies*. Surely, *flutterby* would be a far more accurate and sensible description ... So, she was lying in a verdant meadow, with flowers and butterflies and the sun filtering down very gently through wispy white clouds; the sky blue; a big colourful picnic blanket beneath her, the remnants of her picnic feast in a large wicker hamper with a leather strap standing nearby.

The slightest hint of a warm breeze stirred her soft, clean hair, the scent of her luxury shampoo mixing with that of the meadow flowers and fragrant wild herbs around her. Beyond the blanket, insects went about their business: beetles, ants, ladybirds, a tiny spider—unthreatening, respecting the boundaries of the brightly-coloured fabric, leaving Lucy in peace to enjoy the splendid languor of a beautiful day and a full belly.

As the throbbing in her absent arm subsided and she started to doze, Lucy's still, emaciated form reflected in eight shiny black eyes.

÷

LUCY woke with a start. Someone was pounding on the door—never a good sign. She tried to ignore the banging, but it wouldn't stop. There was still no telling what time of day it was; the darkness in the flat was the same as when she'd fallen asleep. She sat up in bed, anxious and uncertain about what to do. The pounding stopped for a moment and a man's voice boomed from the other side of the door.

"Ms. Aranea!"

It was Les from the Residents' Management Association. It must be the first Monday of the month. *Oh God. The Lottery!*

"Lucy Aranea, open up! I know you're in there!"

"I'm coming. I'm coming!" With considerable effort, Lucy pulled a frayed bathrobe over her threadbare nightie. She opened the front door a couple of inches and peered myopically at the balding, bespectacled man in the corridor.

"You're late," said Les, staring at Lucy through the crack in the door, trying unsuccessfully to see past her into the darkness of her flat. "Everyone's waiting."

"I'm sorry," said Lucy. "Am I the last one?"

"No, I still have a couple more to round up. But you'd better hurry."

Lucy dressed as fast as she could. Despite the months that had passed, she still found operating with one arm difficult, frustrating, and often painful. She locked the door behind her and, holding onto the wall and then the banister, made her ungainly way down the stairs.

The other residents of the building were already waiting in the lobby. At thirteen storeys high, Lucy's building was the smallest on the South Acton Estate. Nevertheless, the vast lobby was filled to breaking point with Lucy's neighbours, standing huddled together like cattle. At one end of the lobby was a concierge's desk—not that there'd ever been a concierge—and seated behind it were three men in suits: Les (in his cheap old suit), a Council employee (in a newish off-the-peg suit), and a representative from a private healthcare company operating in the Borough (in a very expensive tailor-made suit). Had her eyesight been better, and had the occasion been a less sombre one, the comedy aspect of the suit parade would not have been lost on Lucy. As it was, she pondered, as she did on the first Monday of every month: why the theatrics? Why the forced assembly of all the building's tenants, when all of their names were in the Resident Management Association's database and the Lottery draw would all be done on Les's computer in any case? *Theatrics* was probably what it was all about – that, or the so-called "transparency" with which the organisations involved conducted their business.

"Ladies and gentlemen, may I have your attention, please!" There was excitement and a distinct tinge of self-importance in Les's voice as it thundered from the ridiculously vamped-up speaker of his smartphone, startling the people who were standing nearest to him. Without waiting for the nervous chatter to die down, he launched into his usual spiel. "It is my honour and great pleasure to welcome back Mr Bloggs from the Southfield Borough Council, and Mr Botham-Trotter from Happy Health Solutions, for this—the fifty-third Brouncker House Lottery. The winner of this month's Lottery will receive a month's worth of food and water rations and a full medical check-up, and every single Brouncker House tenant will receive one week's rations. I don't need to remind you how very lucky you are to be granted this incredible opportunity thanks to the generosity of Happy Health Solutions."

Les paused to smile sycophantically at Botham-Trotter, then held his hands up high and clapped, turning to his captive audience with an expectant stare and signaling to them to do the same. There was a deafening silence for a moment, then a few people started to clap and eventually the majority of the tenants joined in. Les beamed.

"This month, one lucky resident of Brouncker House will have the privilege of helping a worthy recipient by donating an eye." Les ignored the murmur that echoed around his listeners. "As always, I have all your names here and, at the push of a button, one name will be chosen at random. So, without further ado, I declare the Lottery open."

Silence fell on the crowd once more as Les tapped a button on his phone. Lucy started to feel sick and she zoned out. Her thoughts turned to Lotteries past. To that first time Les had called out her name. She'd been given half an hour to get ready and then she'd been driven in a sleek white vehicle to a resplendent high-tech private hospital on the Fulham Palace Road, owned by Happy Health Solutions, and situated where Charing Cross Hospital had once stood. Grey and a little shabby, Charing Cross Hospital had been free and accessible to everyone who needed healthcare, even housing some fine works of modern art to soothe patients and visitors alike or to stimulate their imagination. The old hospital, like the National Health Service that had run it, was long gone by the time Lucy lost the Lottery (or won it, as Les liked to say), and when she'd woken up in the Happy Health Hospital Nr. 1, following her surgery, Lucy's right kidney was gone.

Fast forward eighteen months, and for 'right kidney' read 'left arm'. There'd been a gasp when those tenants who knew Lucy realised that her name had been picked a second time. Many of them came up to her to commiserate, but some of them congratulated her—genuinely pleased for her or a little jealous that she would have free food and water for a full month, as well as a health check-up.

Lucy still couldn't fathom how society had disintegrated to the point that, in twenty-second-century England, organs were being harvested from living human donors. She hadn't always been poor. As a child, Lucy's parents had been able to pay for her to receive a basic level of education, and she knew about the upheavals that had taken place in twenty-first-century Britain: the civil unrest, the abolition of the monarchy, the collapse of the Union, and the rise of the New Right. But it wasn't until the twenty-second century that

the True Church, the State and the Judiciary had fully merged, erod-
ing basic human rights and widening the division between the haves
and the have-nots. Many medical procedures were banned, and this
included the transplant of animal organs, 3D-printed organs, and
lab-grown organs into humans, on the basis that it was against God's
will. Lucy wondered at the arrogance of people who proclaimed
themselves to know what God wanted. In fact, Lucy wondered
about God.

÷

"LUCY!" A tug on her arm brought Lucy out of her reverie. It was
Jan from down the hall—the lady whose little girl had been born
with no eyes. "You have to go up." Lucy stared at Jan blankly. "Lucy,
you've won!"

"What?" A wave of nausea hit Lucy, stronger than the earlier
one, and light-headedness. She grabbed onto Jan's arm to steady
herself, her gaze falling on Jan's daughter and the skin-covered
hollows where the little girl's eyes should have been.

"Ms. Aranea!" Les's voice reverberated from up ahead. "Please
make your way forward."

Lucy couldn't feel her legs, as though she had somehow detached
from her body, and as the crowd parted before her, she moved
forward on automatic pilot, floating rather than walking. But with
every step, the numbness of shock wore off and the panic set in.

÷

AFTER a week, Lucy had finished her course of antibiotics and
her pain medication had run out. The searing pain in her eye socket
was becoming unbearable again. And there was something moving
under the dressing—Lucy was sure of it. Small, tentative movements. Sometimes painful, sometimes just irritating, but terrifying
nonetheless. Something was growing in the empty space—growing
until the throbbing hollow under the dressing turned into a distinct
bulge.

Finally, Lucy could resist the urge to pick at the fraying dressing no longer. Wracked with pain and fear, she went to the bathroom, where a large shard of mirror still clung to the wall over the sink. *Stupid.* Of course she could see next to nothing in the near dark. Nevertheless, like a zombie shuffling around a shopping mall with some semblance of muscle memory, she stood before the mirror in the darkness as she slowly peeled the dressing from her left eye.

The skin under the plaster holding the bandage in place was raw and itching. As she pulled the dressing away from the side of her nose, revealing the place where her eye had once been, Lucy could hear her own racing heartbeat. Her trepidation turned to horror and confusion, and she cried out, quickly pressing everything back into place.

Lucy couldn't comprehend what had just happened. She stood, breathing heavily, holding the dressing over her eye, waiting for her heartbeat to slow, and thinking. It was as if, for a moment, she'd *seen* something in the mirror. In the darkness. In the impenetrable gloom of her bathroom. Not just something, but the whole bathroom behind her—as bright as day. And a bulging, jet-black eye staring out at her from her own face. From where no eye had a right to be. Phantom pain in her missing arm and occasional twinges in her lower back from where her kidney had been extracted was one thing. But hallucinating an entire eye—and a godawful freaky one at that—was entirely another.

Eventually, Lucy calmed down enough to tackle the dressing once more. And there it was: the eye. Like a small, shiny half-globe in her face, surrounded by her own familiar albeit red and sore skin. An eye blacker than the surrounding darkness. Lucy could see it clearly in the mirror; she could see her own harrowed, furrowed, prematurely-aged face, her skinny body, and her empty, dirty bathroom. She stared at the eye with a mixture of disgust and awe. She tried to close it, but found she had no eyelid with which to blink. She placed her hand in front of the eye and was immediately plunged into darkness. She uncovered the freaky protruding orb again, and closed her normal right eye—now she could see once more. Finally, Lucy opened both eyes and looked around.

*Holy shit.*

Turning back to the mirror, Lucy contemplated her bizarre new eyeball for a bit longer, then smoothed down her dirty, matted hair as best she could and left the bathroom. She walked around her tiny flat, noticing how bare and grimy it was. She'd sold anything of value long ago, to buy food and water. She looked at her stained old mattress in the corner of the bedroom, then up at the large cobweb in the corner above where she'd once had a pillow. The cobweb was there alright—dark with dust and small particles of soot that had crept into the flat through the air vents from the old chimney. But no sign of the spider.

Lucy went to the kitchen and cut a thin slice of bread. She still had three weeks' food and water rations but, with care, she could make them last a lot longer. Her mind had already turned to next month's lottery; she'd have to keep the old bandage and cover her eye with it before going down. With any luck, nobody would notice there was a bulge beneath it rather than a hole.

She was still trying to get her head around her left eye when a stabbing pain assaulted her right one, like someone had plunged a knife into her intact socket and was trying to gouge her eye out. Lucy cried out and doubled over, unable to draw breath. She fell to her knees and that was when something popped and her remaining eyeball fell to the floor in front of her in a gelatinous mess. Her scream came out as a gurgle as she threw up bile, then continued to wretch and hyperventilate until her shaking body finally stilled and she found herself looking at the nightmare before her through two shiny black orbs.

But Lucy's day was just beginning.

By the time it was over, she'd grown six more eyes and six long, thin brown legs, covered with hairs sensitive to sound and smell, and ending with sharp, curved, vice-like claws. Her old legs had retained their pale, fleshy colour, but had stretched and cracked and become long and spindly, ending with claws like the other six. Her segmented body was firm and strong, and her eye-filled head sported a set of disproportionately large, fanged jaws. The only human parts of Lucy that remained were her right arm, mirrored by a hairy brown appendage that had grown from her left stump, and the fast-fading vestiges of her thoughts and memories.

÷

LUCY was exhausted, but strangely calm. Fear, pain, and anxiety had given way to fearlessness, determination, and a sense of clarity she hadn't felt in a long time. But one thing nagged at her: hunger. A voracious hunger, which from now on would be her driving force. She moved effortlessly through the bedroom and inspected the bread, cereal, long-life milk and tinned goods she'd won in the Lottery. She knew instinctively they wouldn't do. Not now that she needed meat and would have to secrete an enzyme to break it down before she could suck it up and digest it. So, what could she eat? And how could she catch it?

Lucy returned to the bedroom and climbed up to the ceiling, the claws at the end of her spindly legs gripping the wall with ease. She peered at the dusty cobweb in the corner, looking for her tiny kin. But there was still no sign of the house spider. Perhaps she was lurking somewhere in the depths of her carefully constructed lair, waiting for prey to come to her. Or maybe she was close to starving, like Lucy soon would be; perhaps languishing in the shadows some-where. Lucy used her human hand and the palp that had grown from her left stump to gently pry apart the threads of the thick, funnel-like web in the corner of the ceiling. Sure enough, at the back of the funnel was the desiccated, lifeless body of the house spider that had been Lucy's sole companion for many months. A fleeting feeling of sadness came over Lucy, metamorphosing quickly into a dogged determination not to meet the same fate. She moved swiftly and gracefully down the wall and through the bedroom to the front door of her flat, which she opened with her human hand, then scurried down the hall to look for her neighbours.

Lucy planned to knock on her immediate neighbour's door, but she paused as the sensitive hairs on her legs picked up the shuffling sound of someone coming down the corridor. Lucy could sense paper scraping against concrete before she saw Mr Trimble. He evidently

had too little energy to lift his feet as he walked, and the old news-
paper he'd tied around them in lieu of shoes made a rough grating
sound as he shambled in her direction. Lucy's hunger intensified and
she moved silently towards her elderly neighbour. But it seemed on
this particular occasion, fate smiled on Mr Trimble. Had he not been
completely blind as a result of a gene mutation triggered by generations of Trimbles raised in the dark, the sight of a human-sized
mutant spider bearing down on him, giant fangs poised to strike,
would probably have caused his heart or a blood vessel in his brain
to give way. As it was, Mr Trimble was spared the horrifying sight of
Lucy's approach. Only the barely audible *clack* of Lucy's claws as she
crept gave away the presence of another living being in the corridor
and, if Mr Trimble heard it at all, he put it down to a rat which had
somehow escaped being captured and eaten by the building's starving inhabitants.

Lucy's hunger increased as she drew closer to the old man. Venom
dripped from her massive fangs, splashing on the bare concrete floor
beneath. As she wondered which part of Mr Trimble she should sink
her fangs into, she suddenly remembered the time he'd smiled at her
when she greeted him in the lobby. Just as quickly, all thought fragments dissipated and brutal instinct kicked in. She surged forward.
And then it hit her—in the chemosensory hairs of all eight legs: the
repulsive smell of poverty and disease; the stench of a living death
only the sick and starving emit. She darted up the wall to avoid collid-
ing with Mr Trimble and scurried towards the stairwell.

Lucy headed for the ground floor of the building, keeping to
the wall, able to cling to the concrete beneath the peeling paintwork
despite her size and weight. The hairs on her legs tingled as she
passed a couple of teenagers sitting on the stairs, drinking some
poisonous home brew made of sewer water and God only knew
what, which would probably have made them blind if government
policy hadn't already done so. Lucy paused, but the smell of sickness
and ketosis coming off them—of bodies forced to digest their own
cells in order to maintain function in the absence of nutrition—
repelled her and she moved on and out of the building.

Twilight had already fallen, but Lucy felt exposed and vulnerable in the open. Ahead of her was the vast wall that separated the South Acton Estate from the Southfield complex, and Lucy instinctively headed for it. High above people's heads, she'd be unnoticed even by the sighted, and she could survey the surrounding area and weigh up her situation without attracting unwanted attention. She began to climb, unaffected by the anti-climb paint, which seemed not to stick to the small surface area of her claws.

Several metres up the wall, Lucy was attracted by the light filtering over the top from the Southfield side. She wanted to perch up there for a while to work out her next move. But there was razor wire and she had a decision to make: stay on the Estate side or navigate the wire. Lucy climbed. Her tapering legs and the claws at their ends were nimble enough to evade the lethal wire. She was momentarily blinded by the lights from the shops and other attractions of the Southfield centre, but soon she was over the top and caught by surprise as her claws sank into the lush vegetation covering the wall on the Southfield side. She stopped for a moment, lifting each of her eight legs in turn, then placing them among the moist leaves once more, savouring the unfamiliar, sumptuous sensation.

Far below Lucy, the shops and restaurants spread like an unfamiliar constellation in a distant part of the world. People, the size of ants from Lucy's vantage point, milled to and fro—strolling along the walkways between the eateries, heading for the mall at the centre of the complex or returning home to their luxury apartments. Lucy watched for a while, the twinkling lights mirrored in each of her eyes. Then she commenced her descent.

Lucy moved slowly, her body barely visible against the dark verdancy of the living wall. She was still metres from the ground when it struck her full force. All the sensors on her legs sparked like lightning, fired up by the hitherto unknown sweet, juicy, plump and wholesome scent of what Lucy immediately recognised to be her destined prey. The sound of laughter and happy, carefree voices pulsated in the tiny hairs on Lucy's legs, and her eyes reflected eightfold her rich, healthy, succulent prey.

As whatever modicum of human sensibility that still remained in her dissipated, never to return, Lucy pounced.

# NGO BINH
# ANH KHOA

## S.A.M.

÷

I glance at my brother when I feel his stare poking at me, demanding that I speak up this time. I blink, passing that burden back to him in a mental ping-pong game that's gone on for the last two minutes or so.

"If you have something to say to me, just say it," a hoarse voice cuts through the air. My attention at once goes back to the speaker on the other side of the coffee table.

Má puts her teacup down. The clink it makes silences all other sounds. She studies us, her eyes intense and unfathomable. Even at the age of seventy, the sharpness of her gaze has not dulled, and against her wordless command, I feel like a little boy again, pinned down by the pressure only a mother could exert. I resist the urge to bow my head. I know my brother feels the same.

Má looks well, but even the best products we've bought for her can't fully hide the wrinkles marring her forehead and the corners of her eyes, or the hints of grayness spreading from the roots of her hair. And yet, she carries herself with utmost grace, just as she's always done when dealing with other people.

Dressed in a tailored *áo dài* of festive red with intricate patterns upon the flapper, woven into elegant lotus flowers in bloom, Má appears as refined as can be for the occasion, a fact that brings us some comfort as her children, but her health is not the main topic that has us tiptoeing around this conversation with her. No, that lies in the company she's keeping.

I force down a sigh and decide to be the bigger man this time, willing my lips to part as my eyes travel from Má to the figure standing behind her, giving her a shoulder rub with a genial smile that makes my skin crawl.

"Má ah," I start and pause a bit to clear the sudden clog in my throat, glad my children are not here to witness this, "What is that thing—"

"Sam," Má cuts in, humming in pleasure.

I click my tongue and push forward. "What is *that thing* doing out here? In the living room? Where anyone can come in and see *it?*"

Má pours herself another cup of green tea. "What's wrong with Sam being out here? He lives here."

"Má, it's a *sexbot!* S.A.M., not Sam! S.A.M.! Sex Assistance Model!" I almost scream, pointing a finger directly at the unnatural face of the robot, a mockery of humanity stretched out in false flesh and plastics. It stares back at me with a tilted head, dark eyes unblinking, the customer-service smile unwavering upon its unblemished mask.

*Also called the S-And-M bot*, a voice growls inside my head, but I don't dare to pronounce it aloud.

"His name is Sam," Má calmly says after a small sip of her drink, her eyes meeting mine without flinching, "And he's a part of this household."

The repressed frustration compels me to lean forward, my arms outstretched and my palms wide open, pleadingly. "Má ah! Aren't you afraid of losing face if anyone sees a glorified sex toy walking around in the open? Heavens above, what if your neighbors see it? You know how they practically live for gossip! What about the uncles and aunties and cousins, huh? Or worse, our wives and children? What will they think of you if they see *it?* What will they think of *us?*"

Silence spreads, shattered only a moment later by the sound of Má's ceramic cup tapping against the table's polished surface. She calls out to the robot by its pet name, and it walks around to the front of

the wood-carved seat, its wavy black hair bouncing with each exaggerated step. And when it sits beside Má, my vision shutters. Personal space hardly exists between the two of them. Má rests a hand upon the bot's, and I feel a sting in my palms as my nails bite into them.

"I fail to see the problem," Má begins, calm as a pond undisturbed by any stray gust of wind. "I'm already in my seventies. My face is not so thin as to grow flustered from the waggling tongues of some clueless outsiders."

"Má, please," my brother says this time, "We're your family, not outsiders."

She simply hums in response, her hand still petting the bot's.

*A routine. A habit.*

A groan escapes my restraint, which dissipates into nothingness like the steam from my untouched tea.

"Family, huh. How nice," Má says, her voice soft and her gaze distant, as though that one word has transported her to a different place. The small upturn at the corners of her lips appears as quickly as it fades away, almost like a mirage. I take a deep breath and close my eyes for a moment, struggling to control the mounted frustration before I part my lips. But some of it still leaks out, and my voice slightly trembles when I speak up.

"Má ah, I know we've not been home for quite some time, but we've been very busy lately. There's always work to be done in our offices. Keeping a job is tough these days, so if we don't work hard, we won't have money to take care of you."

She looks at me with an eyebrow raised.

I fight the urge to bow my head again. I'm no longer a child, but my brain always seems to forget that whenever I talk to her.

"I can live on my pension," she says.

*No, you can't, not in this economy. Subsist, yes. Live, not viable,* I want to retort, but I hold my tongue.

"Má, I know you're lonely, but—"

"I'm not lonely. I have Sam here with me."

The clog in my throat returns, thicker this time.

"If you need company, why not move in with one of us? We would be delighted to have you. Our children like you, too, you know."

Má's other eyebrow briefly joins the first before they both drop. She turns away from me and looks at the family's altar. My gaze trails after hers, taking in the sights of the pictures placed upon the pristine wooden surface—the pictures of our ancestors in black and white, the colored photos of my grandparents, and the latest addition of my father. *Ba*, the word echoes in my brain like a captive banging against his cell, blaring and difficult to ignore. I almost let it out until I remember to take a deep breath and calm down. If I speak the word aloud, the flood of regrets that follows will be catastrophic, and I'm not prepared to deal with that. Not yet.

*The blurry vision is only due to the incense smoke*, I tell myself, blinking repeatedly until my vision returns to normal.

"How can I move away from this home and leave all this behind?" Má says and shakes her head. Moving a person is easy. Moving an entire altar is more complicated, and we all know there aren't many qualified monks left on Earth to perform the necessary rites for the transfer. Má has always been one to uphold the old ways. The old customs, traditions, teachings, and observances, she remembers them all. She embodies them all. And she protects them all, keeping them close to her heart as she was taught to do. Nothing can uproot her from that role, not even her own children.

It's an age-old argument that's always ended in a stalemate, and I don't want to argue about it in front of our ancestors during the sacred Tết holiday, when the family reunion is meant to be joyful and harmonious. I lean back, pinching the bridge of my nose to avoid looking at the way the sexbot's quietly consoling Má with its intimate touches.

My brother knows it's his turn now, and he proceeds with care. "Má ah, we know you feel lonely and want someone to keep you company, so how about we chip in and buy a more suitable robot companion to take care of you when we're not here?"

I nod along. My younger brother's always been the diplomatic one, as befits his station. Má, however, chuckles without mirth at his suggestion, leaning into the bot's embrace.

"Since when are you ever here?" she says in almost a whisper, but she knows we can hear it, loud and clear.

My brother continues, still gentle, still smiling, still coaxing. "I've heard a lot of good things about the latest housekeeping robots. You can choose a butler or a maid model, or even both if you like, and customize their looks and duties as well. They're much better equipped to care for you than, uh, Sam here."

Má scoffs, her fingers still rhythmically tapping on the robot's hand. "I've seen those models before at your fourth auntie's place. Too stiff. Too formal. Too impersonal. You summon them, they come marching toward you like officers with an arrest warrant, and once they're done with their most basic obligations, they just leave you alone in an empty room like a delivered sack of rice without so much as a backward glance. So different from Sam and his more personal diligence."

An S.A.M. bot, per their programmings, can role-play any scene regardless of how long or demanding it is, and excel at catering to its owner's every whim, no matter how unreasonable such whims may be.

*Theoretically, it can even play a role forever.*

I wince at that nauseating thought. How I want to rip out that thing's smiling face, but I can't. The frustration starts building up again, and I notice my fists have, at some point, started shaking upon my lap.

"How about a pet?" my brother carries on, his smile a tad too wide.

Má huffs and says , "I don't like dogs. Too noisy and energetic. I can't chase after them, and I can't clean up after them at this age. And how many cats and hamsters do you think I've buried? My poor heart can't handle more of that. I have no love for birds, pigs, insects, tortoises, rabbits, or geckos, and a fish in a bowl is just another piece of decoration that moves around without any real purpose."

Begrudgingly, I have to respect the way she remembers all the points raised before and shoots them down before they can reemerge. I almost want to suggest a snake just to hear her response.

"Robot pets, then?" my brother says, his voice a bit too loud.

"Where is the fun in taking care of some moving blocks of metal with recycled sound effects?" Má replies, nonchalant.

"Right. How about a robot child? I know a guy who can probably get you one if you want," my brother presses on, ignoring the looks he's receiving.

"You politicians and your bewildering tastes. But no, thanks. I already have real grandchildren. If only they would come for a visit every now and then," Má says, her voice growing pointed toward the end.

"Calling one of the aunties to come and live here with you?" my brother pleads, his words a touch too desperate.

Má snorts at that idea, the barest hint of amusement lacing her tone as she says, "Peh! I can tolerate their presence here maybe three times a month, but dealing with them every day? Please, I'll probably have a heart attack before long. Have you seen how old ladies fight for the only toilet available in a small house? It's brutal. I've seen it. I've *lived* through it. I've no wish to reenact it."

My brother deflates where he sits, shoulders slumping and head down. I wish I could pat his back in sympathy, but a new voice rams into my eardrums, and I feel my face crumpling.

"Má ah, there's a new message for you, from Auntie Lam," the sexbot says with a voice reminiscent of a telesales agent's, its eyes gleaming as it casually captures Má's attention.

"Thank you, dear boy," she replies. I can't remember the last time she spoke that affectionately to me or my brother. And yet, there she is, smiling more freely than I remember her doing as the robot unlocks her phone and clicks on the message for her to read. Whatever she sees seems to delight her.

"Your auntie Lam is handing out lucky money to her cohort of grandchildren," Má says and lets her voice slowly fade away into silence before murmuring, "how nice."

My brother's face is contorted into a grimace, and I'm sure mine is not much different. Má's not even looking at us. Her focus is entirely on her phone and on the bot.

"Má ah—" I say but cannot find the words to continue.

"It's almost time for lunch," the sex toy's insufferable voice says.

"Oh, is it that late already?" Má looks up and checks the time, eyes squinting. She reaches out to pinch the bot's elastic cheek while

muttering to herself about what to eat. The thing's eyes crinkle in simulated joy as it slowly drapes an arm across Má's thin shoulders.

I watch the act and explode.

"Má! Have you no shame! How can you feel fine doing something so uncultured like this?"

Her smile in this instance reminds me of the sunflowers we used to buy during Tết, when my brother and I were still kids. How the flowers once fresh and radiant drooped and withered away by the time the holiday ended. Má's little smile recedes into a thin, straight line as her dark eyes travel back to me. Her posture is as upright as her age allows her to be, and her face just as dignified.

"Shame? I've never done anything that makes me feel shame toward myself or toward our ancestors, both in public and in private."

I can vaguely hear my brother trying to insert himself between us as a buffer, but I don't care. I'm long past caring. My voice rises and fills the incensed air as I spring from my seat. "You're messing around with a sexbot wearing the face of a man my age. If you're like this in front of an audience, who knows what you're up to behind closed doors?"

Má wordlessly regards me before she draws away from the bot. It looks as though it's about to get up and head to the kitchen, but she grabs its hand in a tight grip, making it stay seated.

"I don't have to explain myself or what I do with what's left of my life to either of you, just as you don't need to tell me about what's going on in your lives. But know that at the end of the day, I still have someone by my side to look after these old bones, and know that it's neither one of you."

"That's not true! We're always there for you!"

A wet and sudden laugh is expelled from her throat as she reaches for her walking cane nearby. Without warning, she jabs its wooden end directly at my chest. The tip goes through my holographic projection and makes it glitch.

"How can you be *'there for me'* when you're hardly ever here *with* me, after all these years, even now, even on this day?"

There's no accusation in her tone. And yet, the words cut deep, making both my brother and I jolt. I forget what to say. I even forget how to speak. I could only sit back down, trying to maintain eye contact with her. A futile effort.

"Sam, why don't you go ahead and set the table first? I'll join you soon," I hear her voice wafting through my ears along with the retreating sounds of footsteps.

"Má ah," I start, but my tongue becomes lead. My brother's, too. When I garner enough strength to speak, a new noise tears through the air. A familiar notification that always makes my heart skip a beat. One I specifically set for my senior manager at work. Má knows that, having heard it multiple times throughout the years.

"It appears you are busy, so you'd better go. Both of you," she says, standing up and pressing both hands down on her cane. "You have your duties to tend to, and I have lunch to finish. My doctor tells me to eat three full meals a day, and Sam is making all my favorites today. Your father's as well. Oh yes, I'll have the children's lucky money transferred into your bank accounts in the afternoon. I hope your families will prosper and always be in good health. Happy Lunar New Year, boys."

I reach a hand out toward my smiling mother, and the second my finger almost grazes her back, the connection is cut off from the other side. Má and my childhood home are gone, leaving me alone in the soundproof study in my apartment. My hand still hovers in the air, my fingers outstretched, grasping at nothing.

Before me, the universe stretches seemingly forever onward outside my window, where I try to relocate the familiar shade of blue amid the vast expanse of black and other scattered shades, searching for the home I've left behind some thousand light-years away, all in vain.

Another notification echoes within my hollowness of my study, swallowing the sigh that escapes my loosened lips. Mechanically, I pick up my phone and read the oncoming assault of messages. Duty calls, and rest is a luxury I can hardly afford as of late. Just because I made the cut last time doesn't mean my position is set in stone. I have to keep my job, for there are bills to pay and mouths to feed. I blink repeatedly until my glitching vision becomes clear, and turn toward my laptop, one half of my mind set on tackling the tasks

at hand, the other half wondering what dishes the sexbot (*Sam*, I remind myself) has prepared for Ba and Má. *Is Má's favorite food still the same as the last time I was home?* I don't know.

The familiar clicking sounds fill the space as my fingers race across the keyboard, dragging the majority of my focus back to the flashing screen filled with charts and statistics, but a minuscule portion of my head refuses to be submerged back into that usual domain, in which a memory thought echoes.

*A wish repeated many times may become reality*, Má would often say, back when I was still an only child as she chewed on some left-over vegetables, all the while convincing me she was full. Maybe a lie works in a similar manner. Maybe, if I tell it to myself enough times, I'll be able to see the sexbot (*Sam*, the name reverberates in the back of my mind, uttered by a voice not of my own) as a member of the household like Má can, or, at the very least, I can partake in this prolonged game of pretend, just like we all used to do in the olden days, back when it was so easy to be whoever I chose to be, back when the weight of obligations had not become a suffocating collar. Maybe, if I tell it to myself enough times, I can even paint a smile upon my face in front of the sexbot *(Sam!)* and give it a handshake in front of Má if I ever see it in real life.

Maybe.

Just maybe.

The sounds of the keyboard continue to fill the void, conjuring up the ever-familiar humdrum in which I'm quickly drowned.

# CYNTHIA PELAYO

## THE FIRE OF ROSES

÷

MRS. Darling set off to the grocery store on foot like she did every Tuesday.

The sun beams are bright in the sky after an evening of thunderstorms. She pauses at the end of her front steps and admires her lovely home, with large windows and a wrap-around porch. Beside her is her manicured lawn and her clusters of hydrangeas. There are also pretty tulips in full bloom in neat lines. Tulips are special. A person plants tulips months before they make an appearance. Rain and snow and frost covers them, and all throughout there's patience, waiting, and the knowledge that they'll soon appear.

Yet, all things creep to the surface.

However, what are Mrs. Darling's gems are her rich, fiery red climbing roses she has positioned on trellises against her home. These were planted a long, long time ago by Mrs. Darling's grandmother and loved and cared for by her mother and now Mrs. Darling herself.

Mrs. Darling loves her home, and she loves her garden, but it's those roses that bring her the most joy because they remind her not just of this house but this town and how important it is to keep everything beautiful and pristine. She scans her property once more with a so much joy. Her eyes fall over to Mrs. Rodgers' house, and there's a pinch in her chest. The peach paint is flaked and peeling, the lawn is overgrown and burnt at the ends from a lack of watering. No longer is there the kaleidoscopic burst of colorful tulips. Where they once stood, weeds dominate. After Mr. Rodgers died, Mrs. Rodgers seldom leaves her house. It was in leaving her house to run a quick errand when Mr. Rodgers died, and the guilt has eaten her up since, just like the weeds have eaten up her once beautiful front garden. Still, at least they had a home nurse who helped keep Mr. Rodgers as comfortable as possible during his final days.

Mrs. Darling knows everyone in her town.

She knows their names, and their movements. Mrs. Darling knows where each of them live. She also knows when each of them arrived in this town. She has lived here all her life, just like her mother and her mother's mother. Of course, she is fond of strangers and tourists who visit in summer months, those who stop into the Fudge Shoppe or the Main Street Bakery before making their way down to the lovely beach to enjoy the glimmering lake.

Mrs. Darling is seventy-four years old and whenever she'd run into a stranger or a tourist in town she would point and say, "My grandfather and grandmother lived there. That is the very first house built in this town."

Today that house serves as the town post office, and a reminder of sorts of how far this town has come.

Mrs. Darling would then go on to tell them a little bit about all the things her grandfather and grandmother did to settle this town. Her grandmother especially worked hard to keep this town right and beautiful and pristine as new families moved in. One must pay close attention to those who live around them, their neighbors and their friends. Mrs. Darlings pays close attention to all the people, when she visits the library and the park and the post office and the grocery store and the doctor's office and more.

Mrs. Darling is always listening.

She also listens to the strangers and the tourists. Mrs. Darling would also point out to the strangers and the tourists the roses surrounding the courthouse and tell them how her grandmother planted those herself. Roses are hearty and long lasting, just like Mrs. Darling, just like her town. Red roses symbolize achievement, perfection and more. That is what this town meant to Mrs. Darling, and she did what she could to protect it.

Sometimes the strangers and the tourists would ask Mrs. Darling about the beautiful, velvety roses outside her home since there were so many of them, asking if they could take some. Yet, Mrs. Darling did not feel comfortable with her beautiful blooms being taken off to strange towns. The roses belong to this town and to Mrs. Darling.

Once, Mrs. Darling was asked if she would like to share some of her roses as decoration for the tables at the community picnic. Instead she sent over a basket of fresh baked rolls.

Reaching Main Street now, Mrs. Darling finds herself stopping every few minutes and saying hello to another resident of her town. They give warm smiles and hellos, good mornings and bits of conversation. Soon she reaches the grocery store and there it is the same, knowing everyone and sharing greetings.

"Good morning, Mrs. Darling," Mr. Jones says.

"It is such a perfect morning, now isn't it, Mr. Jones," Mrs. Darling says.

The Jones family has two teenage children, Lilly and Ryan. They each attend the town's high school. Both spend a lot of time online. Lilly shares videos of make-up tutorials, and Ryan streams himself playing video games. The children do this for hours and hours, interacting with their parents at minimum, their world the space of the screen capturing their movements and the comments and the emojis that flood in. Mr. Jones is here to purchase groceries and, as always, Mrs. Darling asks Mr. Jones how Mrs. Jones is doing.

"Oh, she's doing great," he says, and Mrs. Darling smiles knowing this is a lie because she never sees the family members together.

Mrs. Darling gathers all her ingredients—bread and cheese, a chicken to roast this evening—and items to bake a tart, and tea to enjoy throughout the day.

Mrs. Darling sets her groceries down on the conveyor belt and one by one Timothy scans them.

"Good morning, Mrs. Darling," Timothy says.

"Good morning, Timothy," Mrs. Darling says as she watches him carefully scan and bag her items. "How is your father?"

Without making eye contact, Timothy says, "Fine," but Mrs. Darling knows Timothy's father Ronald is not fine at all, not after he had gotten into an ugly fight last night when his car bumper was struck in the parking lot of this very grocery store.

Ronald's anger was so much so that as the driver apologized profusely for the mistake, Ronald punched him in the face, breaking his nose. In fact, Mrs. Darling noticed there were still splatters of blood in the parking lot that hadn't been cleaned. She didn't like that at all. Mrs. Darling knows all these things and more.

"That's good," Mrs. Darling says. "And your mother?"

Timothy gives Mrs. Darling her total and then he says, "My mother's fine too."

Mrs. Darling smiles and replies, "That's good to hear," even though she knows Timothy's mother lost her job this morning after missing yet another shift at the restaurant, this time to collect her husband from jail.

Carrying her groceries, Mrs. Darling meets Linda and Steve right outside the grocery store, a young couple with a baby, Evelyn. Little Evelyn wears a white dress with a pretty, white embroidered cap.

"That young child is going to always expect the finest things," Mrs. Darling says.

"She's my princess," Linda says.

"Princesses get into trouble sometimes," Mrs. Darling says.

"I'm worried about her," Linda says. "Shouldn't she be able to sit up by now? What if there's something wrong with her?"

"Would it matter? It's your daughter?" Mrs. Darling says, trying to read Linda's expression. People say so much about what they feel with their micro-expressions.

Linda shakes her head. "Of course not."

Mrs. Darling nods, but she knows what she reads on Linda's face, the early markings of something so sinister. Critique and ridicule and abuse first lingers in questions.

"You should probably apologize to her," Mrs. Darling says.

Linda's eyes widen. "Excuse me?"

Mrs. Darling waves to the baby and says firmly, "To your daughter. You should apologize to your daughter for how you feel."

Linda nods. "Right," she says, before turning to Evelyn and saying, "I love you, my princess. You're perfect just the way you are."

On her way home with her groceries, Mrs. Darling sees teenagers Margaret and Darla. Darla is crying, and Mrs. Darling suspects she knows what their fight was about. She had seen Margaret just the other day with Nora. Margaret and Nora were getting close, it seemed, and Darla did not like this. That is how jealousy works. It is a nasty little thing that laces itself around and around and tightens, and today Mrs. Darling sees it tightening around Darla's neck.

As Mrs. Darling approaches her house, she can smell her rich, perfect roses positioned against her neat and perfect house in this neat and perfect town. She stops with her groceries in hand and thinks about perfection. Perfection must be actively maintained, and as her grandmother had done, she will continue to do.

Mrs. Darling's thoughts then drift to people disturb her with the things they do, and the things they say, and their little wicked micro-expressions that appear just for a second but tell the truth about what they think and how they feel about things and others. And people often hurt each other, doing so frequently, either not knowing or not caring.

The scent of roses increases and Mrs. Darling moves quickly. She pauses in front of her home and admires how the climbing roses stretch up and across the trellises. They look so beautiful, these full red bursting blooms.

Inside, Mrs. Darling puts away her groceries. So many thoughts run through her mind. She is no longer hungry. She will eat later. For now, she will make a cup of tea and sit at her desk and write one of her letters. This is what she does. This is what she likes to do, write her letters, because it is in writing these letters that she keeps her town clean and pristine. This is what she learned from her mother, and her grandparents.

She takes out her special white stationary and her special white envelopes and her special pen. Her stationary has gold trim and once the letters are written she finishes them off with a gold-colored seal, with the image of a rose.

The first letter is for Mr. Jones and in it, she tells him that his children hated him and their mother and, as a matter of fact, their mother was diagnosed with cirrhosis of the liver, as overheard the other day in the doctor's office. Yet it appears his wife continues to drink, perhaps because she hates him and hates her life with him and her children so much she wants it over. As always, Mrs. Darling doesn't sign the letter, but she seals it and places it in the envelope and soon off it would go to the post office.

She writes the next letter to Timothy's mother, and in it she tells the woman how unfortunate it is that she lost her job and had to bail her husband out of prison, but that sadly it will happen again because her husband has raging anger issues. Everyone in town knows this and everyone is afraid of him. He may even kill someone one day because of it, maybe even her. This letter is sealed and off it would go as well.

More letters are written. One to Linda, criticizing her mothering skills, questioning if she even loves little Evelyn. Another letter is for Steve, alerting him that he should probably watch Linda carefully around young Evelyn, because there is suspicion that Linda wants to harm the child, and one could picture this wicked mother smothering her daughter in the night and blaming it on too many blankets in the crib later. The letter is sealed.

Mrs. Darling smiles to herself and then writes one more letter she had been wanting to write to Mrs. Rodgers next door. In it, she tells Mrs. Rodgers that yes, her suspicions are that Mr. Rodgers did die painfully and alone, because the nurse on duty, Margaret's mother, said so and left her shift early to attend to her daughter's romantic quarrel with Darla, and for fifteen minutes Mr. Rodgers writhed in pain as their home nurse abandoned him, leaving him to reach to the nightstand alone for his pain medicine, eventually falling out of bed and knocking his head and dying.

Mrs. Darling is pleased with the quality of her letters today. This batch will help maintain the cleanliness of her town. She finishes her cup of tea and gathers her letters and walks down to Main Street and places the letters into the mailbox.

Mrs. Darling hears crying and shouting behind her and there are Margaret and Darla, once again in a public lover's quarrel.

She shuffles away quickly, bothered by the professions of love from one and apologies from the other. What Mrs. Darling doesn't realize is that one of the letters falls to the ground and as she leaves Darla picks it up.

"What's that?" Margaret asks.

Darla rubs her eyes. "It's addressed to your mom," she says, handing it off to Margaret.

Margaret takes it in her hand. "What? Give me that."

Later that night, Mrs. Darling works away in the kitchen, preparing her roast and her tarte. She feels very good about her day today, all the conversations she had and all the conversations she listened to. It is important to know the movements of everyone and where things must be cleaned and refined. This is her duty, to maintain the decency of her little society, of her little world, and she will continue doing so until her very last day.

There is a knock on the door and Mrs. Darling is surprised to have a visitor so late. She wipes her hands on her apron, opens the front door, and finds no one there, but there is a letter. She kneels to retrieve it when the trellises on either side of her house burst into flames, shooting up over the house. Flames erupt along the doorframe, forcing Mrs. Darling back into her house. She screams, falling onto the hardwood floor. She scrambles to her feet and rushes to her phone to dial the fire department, the letter still in her hand.

As she dials, the letter slips out of the envelope. It reads:

*I hope you enjoy the fire your roses bring.*

# ELIZABETH MASSIE

## TWO SCHOOLS

÷

THE typed note left under Principal Sam Denny's office door was simple enough.

"I wish we didn't have Ms. Casales for a principal. I wish we had a good one like you."

Sam smiled a curious smile as he eased into his wingback chair and flipped the paper over to see if it had been signed. It hadn't. Clearly it was from a student at Piedmont, the elite sister school to Sam's institution, Blue Ridge Tandem Private School.

"It doesn't really matter who wrote it," Sam said to himself. He carefully folded the paper and slipped it into his top desk drawer. "And of course, I am the best." It was amusing, hearing his words aloud, though he knew it was true.

Sam had a wonderful reputation at Blue Ridge Tandem. The students, staff, and parents loved him. He'd served as Tandem's principal for forty-six years. Under his wisdom and care, he had increased student success to where, as small as Tandem was, for the last seven years had been listed as one of the top ten private schools in the nation.

Yet it seemed at least one student over the mountain at Piedmont Private School was struggling to get used to their new principal, twenty-seven-year-old William and Mary graduate Angeles Casales. She'd taken the job after

Piedmont's long-time principal and Sam's friend, George Wilson, had been killed in a boating accident over the summer. Casales had taken the job in early September. It was now mid-October.

Out the window, Sam could see the school's soccer field and beyond that the Tandem stable. The girls' team was practicing on the field, fresh and bright in their uniforms of red and white. The boys' team would practice after lunch. Sam enjoyed watching the teams. He couldn't be prouder of his students' accomplishments, both intellectually and athletically. Tandem had been serving the best of the best since 1893, and the standards to which it held were impeccable.

A knock on the office door. Sam's secretary, Bella Schuman, poked her head in. "Mr. Bloom wanted to check and see if you'll be observing his biology class next period."

"Of course, I'm on my way in just a moment."

Bella nodded, drew back and closed the door.

Sam watched one of the girls kick a goal and her team surround her with hugs. "Thank you, God, for these students, this school, my job," he whispered his daily prayer. "I will never let it, or you, down."

The majestic backdrop to the field and the stable was the rise of the Blue Ridge Mountains, currently bathed in autumn shades of yellow and orange. Piedmont Private School was thirteen miles away, over on the eastern side of the mountains. Not quite as highly-ranked as Tandem (it came in at number twelve), Piedmont was still revered as a prime example of top-notch education for high school students. Tandem and Piedmont considered themselves "sister schools," and engaged in challenging but good-natured competitions, basking in the successes of each other, upholding their glowing reputations. The teachers of both schools enjoyed each other's company and gathered several times a year for "Duel-Faculty" events. Students from both schools were frequently best friends and it wasn't unusual to see them together in the winter, skiing at Winterglow on the western ridge of the mountains or going to movies in the eastern town of Nelson.

Sam rubbed his eyes—almost constantly watery now with age—and wondered what Angela Casales was really like. He'd seen her photo in the Piedmont newsletter and she looked energetic and

bright. He hoped she would do well, though George Wilson had mighty big shoes to fill.

Pulling himself up, Sam paused against the pain in his knee then headed out to the science lab.

$$\div$$

TO: Hilly Anderson:

I'm texting from Biology class. Old hard-nose Denny's observing. We're, like, making stupid worms go thru T-mazes. Zzzzzzz

Sounds Zzzzz. Hey Joanie U get the note to Denny without anybody seeing?

Yeah under his office door early this morning. step one done

Tonight I'll send U something else to give him in the morning

Sounds good

I'm in algebra now. Zzzzzz

Fuck hate math

Our plan's more fun than math or worms

Fuck yeah

Denny will get Casales fired she's such a bitch.

Happy to help get that done

Gotta go bye Joanie, Mitchell lookin over
at me


Bye Hilly


÷


SAM Denny walked home from school at 6:42, late but not later
than usual. His house was on campus and there was no need to rush.
He had no one waiting his wife, Betty, had passed away at home
three years ago, following an exhausting, messy case of Alzheimer's.

At home on his living room sofa, Sam sipped a small glass of
orange juice and blotted his watery eyes with a tissue. His knee
throbbed. He'd have to get in touch with Doctor Bob soon for more
help. He rubbed his knee carefully then took an evening vitamin.
From the kitchen, he could smell the pasta sauce he'd set to simmer-
ing. It was own recipe, which he'd share to much acclaim with the
sister school faculties at one of the Duel Faculty gatherings. He was
a superb cook, be it pasta or potato salads or cakes or you-name-it.
Made him extra proud.

On the mantle over the fireplace were two framed documents.
His diploma from Tandem, dated fifty-three years earlier, and his
master's diploma from the University of Virginia. He smiled, feeling better now, and took another sip of orange juice. What could be
more rewarding than spending one's life molding and directing young
people into a well-structured, well-educated life? So much bad was
going on in other schools across the nation. Disrespect, drugs, bully-
ing, violence. Dreadful. But at Tandem and Piedmont, young minds
were being carefully prepared to responsibly take up the reins of a
country in need. Sam knew all the students here and most at Piedmont. There was not a one he wouldn't vote for if they ran for office.

Sam poured more orange juice, made his way to the kitchen, and
settled down at the spotless table for dinner.


÷

÷

TO: Joanie Lawson:

A picture's attached. When I was in Spanish I went to the bathroom and looked out the hall window and saw sophomore Kate Spilman hiding between cars in the faculty parking lot. She was, like, smoking! She has dark hair a lot like Casales'. I took a shaky photo that if U didn't know better you'd think it was Casales suckin up the nicotine! HA!

Cool, Hilly! Nobody supposed to smoke at school!

Print it out and write something good on it.

I will. Denny will hate seeing Casales breakin rules. Christ he loves rules more than life. I'll put it under his door tomorrow

Make sure he wont see U

I'll be careful

With our plans I bet Denny'll get Casales will be fired before Halloween! She's such a snotty bitch, let her get a job sweeping floors somewhere

We Tandem girls will always look out for Piedmont girls. Happy to help

÷

÷

IT was a rainy morning. Sam had orange juice, an apple, and a vitamin for breakfast then left home with his trusty umbrella and briefcase, his knee and his mood so much better. He strolled the walkway to the administration building, humming "Singin' in the Rain." He liked that song. All was right with his world. All was right with his job. How many people could say that?

He entered the building, put the umbrella in the community umbrella stand, then walked down the hall to his office. It was early. Miss Schuman, his secretary, wouldn't be in for another twenty minutes. That was good. He liked the quiet of no voices and the comforting, occasional creak of the old floors and walls.

Once again, he found a folded sheet of paper on the floor inside his office door. He frowned, took it to his desk, and put on his reading glasses. He'd need new ones soon, but what he saw was clear enough. It was a photo, printed out in black and white, showing a blurry, dark-haired female in the Piedmont faculty parking lot, smoking a cigarette. A note at the bottom read: "Photo taken yesterday afternoon. Principal Casales was hiding in the parking lot so nobody knew she was smoking."

No, no.

Sam's jaw clenched; his lip hitched. To ignore the regulations of either school was inexcusable. Ms. Casales needed to clean up her act immediately if she was going to keep her job. What to do?

Sam took off his glasses and looked out the office window. Frank, one of the property's maintenance men, was down in the hockey field, mowing the grass. The last mow of the season. Beyond that, the riding instructor was grooming a horse in the corral outside the stable, preparing for the eight o'clock riding lessons. The mountains were clothed in clouds.

Who sent this photo? Well, that was much less important that what the photo revealed.

What to do?

÷

Wednesday October 22nd.

Dear Ms. Casales,

I'm sure you are familiar with the student and faculty handbooks. There are certain things that are forbidden on campus. It has come to my attention that you have been smoking in the Piedmont parking lot. Rather than bring that to the attention of your school's governing board, I'm asking you privately to never smoke on campus again. Our schools have unblemished reputations that we are sworn to uphold. In fact, I'd suggest you stop smoking altogether. For parents to see you doing so off campus would also become an issue.

Thank you for your kind attention and I'm sure you understand.

Samuel Denny,
Principal, Blue Ridge Tandem School.

TO Hilly Anderson:

Hey Hilly. Denny got the photo. I saw him this morning in the hallway he looked pissed. He never looks pissed like that. I think UR plans gonna to work. Time to up it some.

Good thanks Joannie. I am working on a new note will send it to U after school. In Government class right now. Cant write much. But yeah, I'm gonna make sure Casales is fired soon. I hate her she thinks shes all that! Bitch! Shit I gotta go bye

÷

THE school library was the most studious place on campus. Sam loved walking through, watching students bent over books or notebooks or laptops on long, century-old wooden tables. It was quiet; peaceful. It smelled of books, a grand heritage, order, tradition, and the quest for knowledge. What it did not smell like was cigarette smoke. Sam nodded at the librarian, Mrs. Kirk, and she nodded back. Boys and girls glanced up then went back to work.

The note he'd written to Ms. Casales had been sent in a sealed envelope via the Tandem-Piedmont mail service. She would have the letter this afternoon. That should be the end of it. Sam would have kept Piedmont on the straight and narrow without anyone else knowing of her terrible transgression. The sister school kingdom was safe.

÷

THE following morning. Sam arrived at his office to find an envelope slipped under his office door.

Again?

As he picked it up, he wondered if he should have a secret camera set up to see who was passing these messages? But then he thought, No. If he did that, and the clandestine message-sender found out, Sam might lose vital information about Ms. Casales.

He told Bella Schuman he wasn't to be disturbed as he had calls to make. She nodded and turned her attention back to her computer.

Door closed, Sam sat and slowly opened the envelope. Maybe it was a private reply from Ms. Casales?

But it wasn't. The note read:

"Two nights ago, Ms. Casales had some of the senior boys over to her house. They stayed for hours. Not sure what they do in there but it's weird, don't you think? I know because I've started watching her secretly and taking notes. I'm worried. Can you help? Shouldn't she be fired? Can you make that happen?"

No no no!

This was quite disgusting, very bad, worse even than smoking. Sam's heart picked up a painful rhythm. He pulled the September school newsletter from the bookshelf behind his desk. It contained the usual who-did-whats-over-the-summer, new student profiles, a whole page dedicated to the sister school's former and now deceased principal, George Miller, and then a brief welcome to Angela Casales, George's replacement. Sam stared at Casales' headshot. Fair-looking young woman, but one who either scoffed the school's traditions or was clueless beyond belief. She was a threat to Piedmont and by association, Tandem. She had to go. But he couldn't share that information. The talk that would follow, the questions, the suspicion regarding the schools' abilities to make proper leadership choices would cloud both schools like fog on the Blue Ridge. After more than one hundred years, the reputations would come tumbling down because of one woman.

The one thing he would not do was tell on her to have her fired. God, what to do?

The letter he composed was written in furious, shaky handwriting. It was quite to the point and in a nutshell:

> *Do not EVER under any circumstances invite or allow students into your home. I mean it, Ms. Casales!*
> *— Samuel Denny, Principal, Tandem School.*

The note went into an envelope and immediately into the sister school mail system.

÷

TO Joanie Anderson:

Damn. Friday afternoon and Principal Casales still here still struttin her shit in the halls.

I guess Denny hasn't had time to do anything yet

Yes he has! Fuck this. He gotta get her fired
quick. I hate her stupid smile

          A couple more nudges will do it I know be
          patient Hilly

I'll send U something really good over the
weekend for U to give Denny on Monday

          U mean something really bad

Ha! but yeah. Lunch just rang. Meatloaf today.
Hate meatloaf with a passion bye Joanie

          Bye Hilly

÷

SAM slept very over the weekend. He'd mind was all over the place, trying to determine if there was something more he could do to make sure Ms. Casales knew her place. He thought of inviting her to lunch on Saturday to give her a very stern talking to. But then again, perhaps by now, having read his most recent correspondence, she had realized she had to change her ways. That's what he prayed for. His knee hurt worse than usual. He took an additional vitamins to help, but it was basically useless.

÷

TUESDAY morning, there was a letter in Sam's administration box, not under his office door. The envelope had Piedmont's return address but no name. Whoever was sending these important messages had clearly decided another means of communication was safest. That was good.

    The letter read:

*Principal Casales had two more senior boys into her
house Sunday night. And creepy van showed up at
her place when it was dark. She came outside laughing and holding a cigarette. She got something from
the driver. Looked like a little packet of something.
I saw this through the front yard hedges. I only
spied because I love being a student at Piedmont
and Principal Casales shouldn't be in charge. Please
do something, Principal Denny. There is no one at
Piedmont I can confide it. Our school needs you!*

Sam crushed the note.

Oh, dear God!

"Dear God, what to do?" he shouted.

A tap on the door. Bella stuck her head in. "Sir, did you call me?"

Sam shook his head and forced a smile.

"Are you feeling all right?"

Sam nodded. "Of course."

"All right, sir, let me know if you need anything."

"I will."

The door closed. Panic squeezed Sam's torso like a straightjacket. He fumbled for the phone, his rotary from his early years in this job.

But then, as he lifted the receiver, he whispered, "Who are you going to call? There is no one! Don't be stupid! If anyone else learns about her abuse, word gets out. Word gets out and information flies free like a raptor. And there's no calling it back. Then Piedmont is ruined. If Piedmont is ruined, Tandem is ruined as well, because if this kind of thing happens at one, surely it must happen at both. Reporters, furious parents, tearing us down. Destroying us."

He slammed the receiver down.

"Yet if I don't tell someone, students are in danger!"

God in Heaven, what on Earth to do?

He looked out the window at the mountains. They offered no help, no suggestions.

The phone rang.

Sam wiped his forehead. He counted his breaths. "Slow down, Sam," he said. "I'm smart. I'll figure it out. I'll make it right. Put on your principal hat."

He answered the phone. "Principal Denny speaking."

The voice was even, cold, adult, female. "Principal Denny, this is Principal Casales over at Piedmont. I've read your accusations. They are completely and utterly unfounded. You've never even met me. How dare you, sir. You need to stop. I hope I'm making myself clear."

"I ... we need to ..." began Sam.

"No, we don't," said Casales. "I know you miss George Miller. But I'm here now. I plan on staying. I love this school and I'm working for the students best interests. Don't ever even consider sending one of your twisted messages again. Do you hear me?"

"I ..."

"Do you hear me?"

Sam couldn't speak.

The phone line went dead.

A rush of rage slammed Sam in the chest. This pedophile, drug addict smoker would not get away with this.

He would make sure of that. He would save the day. And he would do it alone.

$$\div$$

TO Hilly Anderson:

> Hey girl Denny is really messed up. Walking the halls not saying hi to anybody like he used to. Looks more than pissed for sure. If he hasn't called the Piedmont board yet I bet he will now!

> I fuckin hope so. U know Casales' is making us follow all the damn rules? She's young she should know we don't want to do all that shit like we had to under Principal

Wilson. She gave me a fuckin tardy slip this morning. Casales saw me coming out the bathroom and, like, jumped on my case. Fuck I was only fixing my eyeliner.

I dunno what else U can do, Hilly.

Hey we gonna have that sister school Halloween party is this Friday. This year it's in our school gym. We should sneak out from the party and fuck up her office somehow just for fun

Would love that!

I will. But damn, Denny gotta get her fired and soon.

I never asked U by why U want Denny to get it done?

Because hes like Principal Wilson was, an old fart with the power to get her ass kicked to the curb.

Okay talk to U later

Bye

÷

THE sister school Halloween party had been a tradition since the late 1950s. The schools took turns hosting the celebrations in their gyms, which included a costume contest (no sexy nurse or other suggestive outfits allowed), a huge snack table piled with Halloween sweets, concert of music provided by school bands, challenging games of knowledge with prizes, and a pumpkin carving station. All well-chaperoned, all well-attended. Students each year had asked the staff to include a dance but that was never given the green light. Nobody pushed it though because staff had final say and rules were rules.

This year's celebration was held at Piedmont.

Many of the teachers and other staff members dressed for Halloween, too, though they didn't take part in the contest. They did it because it added to the festive mood of the evening. Even George Wilson had donned clever outfits like a mailman or pilot. Sam never was comfortable stepping out of line, so always went as a private school principal, which consisted of his usual clothing with a name tag reading, "Private School Principal."

It was late afternoon and quite cold. The Halloween party was tonight, and Sam had volunteered to help set up. It would also give him the chance to do what needed to be done to save the schools. "God help me," he said as donned his coat, scarf, and leather gloves then climbed into his car. "And I know you will. For the greater good, Lord." He started the engine.

A gift for the new principal was on the seat, wrapped in appropriate Halloween-orange paper. A tag on the box read "From an old friend at William and Mary. Congrats on your position at Piedmont."

Sam could barely constrain his uncomfortable excitement. He drove out of the Tandem parking lot and took Route 250 over the colorful, cheerful mountains.

÷

TO Joanie Anderson:

> I finally decided on my costume gonna be a
> goon

>> Not too scary or they wont let U get into
>> the gym.

Like I dont know that, going to Piedmont 4 years now. What about U?

Cheerleader but not sexy got pompoms on Amazon.

Party starts at 7:30 Meet in the gym then. We'll go to the west hall bathroom and when the janitor's done cleaning Casales' office we'll sneak in there and fuck that place up. When she sees it she'll be, like, majorly pissed but wont tell anybody cause she doesn't want anybody to know some kids hate her. Then Monday I'll send another note to Denny about something bad, I'm not sure what I'll say yet. But after that Principal Denny'll have to meet with the Piedmont board and tell em about her smoking and drugs and having kids in her house. She'll be kicked out and she'll be sorry she was such a cunt.

U bet see U at 7:30

÷

SAM passed through the Piedmont security gate and waved at Jose who manned the gate. Both Piedmont and Tandem had such security, along with tall stone walls around the property. But that was all that was needed. There were no armed guards, no cameras in the hallways like public schools. That would ruin the historic ambience, would suggest that within the property boundaries, students and staff were not safe.

Driving up the winding drive through the maples and autumn gardens, Sam reached the main building and parked as close to the front door as possible. Like Tandem, the school consisted of several red brick buildings, classic style, erected in the late 1890s. Piedmont had a clock tower that Tandem didn't, though Tandem did boast an old carriage house.

Sam tucked the gift for Angeles Casales under his jacket and climbed from the car. He kept his elbow pressed to his side so the package wouldn't slide down. He went in the arched front doorway and headed down to the gym.

The maintenance crew had almost finished polishing the floor, and several of the teachers were lining the walls with chairs. Another teacher was on the stage, checking the sound system for the music that would be part of the celebration. Students of the Tandem Art Club were taping paper pumpkins and ghosts and witches and tombstones wherever there was room to tape. Sam wasn't fond of Halloween; he didn't like the idea of witches and ghosts decorating either school. But it had been a tradition, it had been acceptable since the 1940s and so he went along with it. He respected the wisdom of those who came before him.

Sam glanced around, hoping Principal Casales was not there. He knew that, traditionally, the principals would meet with the guidance staff every Friday afternoon, and it looked like that was the case now. She was most likely in the library.

Good.

"Sam!" It was the world history teacher, Mike Riley. He was setting up the snack table. "So good to see you! We sure can use your help!"

"I'll be right with you. Just need a little visit to the washroom."

"Sure."

Sam knew where the principal's office was, naturally. He'd visited his George Wilson many times here. They'd shared countless stories of school days gone by as well as fresh tales of academic adventures. Glancing around to make sure no one was nearby, Sam peeked into Casales' secretary's nook. The room was empty.

Thank you, God.

He quietly moved across to Casales' office and reached for the doorknob. His hands sweated in the gloves. Surely, Casales was in the library. But if she were here, he could certainly talk his way around it, and even confront her about her behaviors in person. He was a professional.

He turned the knob, pushed the door open. Casales was not there. He went inside.

His jaw began to chatter, which was so unlike him. But a situation like this was so unlike Piedmont. So wrong. So horrible. So in need of decisive action.

He pulled the gift from his jacket. It rattled a little. Inside were a dozen pumpkin shaped, vanilla-iced cookies that Sam had baked the day before. Baked with a special something crushed into powder and worked into the batter and stirred into the icing for good measure.

Letting out a shuddering breath, Sam hobbled from the office and down the hall. The ache in his knee was returning.

Back in the gym, he joined Mike at the snack table. "Let me help you there," he said, approaching. "I'll slice the carrot cake."

"Sure," chuckled Mike. "But for heaven's sake, take off those gloves first."

÷

TO Joanie Anderson:

> Hey gurl where are U? Its, like, 7:45. The party started already and U aren't here yet.

> > Sorry, Hilly. My car was almost out of gas so I had to stop at the station and get a few gallons. I'm almost at Piedmont now, though. Fifteen minutes at the most.

> Whatever

÷

THE gym clock read 7:53. Sam hung back by the gym's rear exit, trying to avoid Principal Casales. She's come into the gym before the party started. Clearly, she'd not visited her office after her library meeting.

She was quite lovely in real life, there in her black slacks and white blouse. But Sam could see through the façade to the demon she actually was. Certainly, she'd seen him after all this time but hadn't approached him. Maybe she thought to cut him some slack. No, no. The she-demon was playing with him like a cat and a bug, knowing he wouldn't call her out in public.

Even though the party was barely underway, Sam had had enough. He couldn't tolerate being there any longer. He followed Mike Riley over to the stage and told him his knee was killing him (not a lie) and needed to go home. Mike told him no problem, just having Sam there to help a bit was a treat. Sam hurried as best he could from the gym and out of the school. He could see the darkened window of Casales' office. Surely, she'd stop in there before going home after the party. She had to. Then things would be right again.

Back in his car, back on the road. Sam took the dark, two-lane road across the Blue Ridge. He dry-swallowed a vitamin from his glove compartment. There were only three left, though. Tomorrow night, he would need to trek to the home of his human savior, Doc Watkins. The good doctor work worked privately and discreetly out of his back room in Nelson. He sold Sam all the vitamins he needed, as many as he needed, whenever he needed them. They not only killed the pain but also made Sam feel better overall for a while. Sure, they cost a fortune but were worth it.

What was also worth it was the vial of white pills Doc gave Sam when he told the good doc about Principal Casales. The doc said the pills were very popular these days, fenta-something. They could be swallowed whole or, as Sam had hoped, crushed into powder. They weren't the same kind of pills the doc had given Sam for Betty. But Doc Watkins had assured Sam that the results would be the same. Fairly quick. He didn't say painless but wasn't that almost the same thing as quickly?

Thank goodness Sam had a spotless reputation. All would be well.

÷

TO Joanie Anderson:

It's already 8. I couldn't wait any longer cause Janitor Kyle would be gone and we'd be locked out. I sneaked down the dark hall and saw Kyle going in and out of Casales' office. When he went out again to dump trash in the big container I slipped into the office and hid in her closet. Kyle came back one last time then left and locked the door. When U get here knock quiet and I'll let U in.

Done any messing up her office yet?

Not yet I was waiting for U, Joanie. It's no fun doing that alone. Its dark in here but there's enough light from outside to see. Hey! There's a box on her desk. From some old friend back at college. Lemme take a peek. Iced Halloween cookies! They look really good. I'm eating one. Fuck it's good! I claim six. U get six and Casales won't get shit. Hurry up or I'll eat yours, too.

Ha! See you in a few.

# JOHN F.D. TAFF

## YARD SIGNS

÷

IT had been about a week since the last upgrade.

Dale heard the phone ring, and it jarred him. Even more than the continual rumble of fighter jets overhead, the roar of fires outside, and distant explosions.

The phone had rang often, as it usually did during a big election season, though it hadn't rung in a day or two.

He knew exactly why it *hadn't*.

Just as he was sure he knew exactly why it *was* ringing now ...

... and exactly what the voice on the other end of the line would offer.

A final upgrade.

÷

THE sign in the neighbor's front yard was for *that* guy.

Dale hadn't noticed it before, and he would've noticed any sign for that guy, anywhere in his entire neighborhood. He wasn't surprised it would be in his neighbor's yard. The husband was a college professor and his wife owned a hot yoga studio, whatever that was.

No, Dale was only surprised it had taken this long for them to put up a sign. Dale had tried, oh yeah, he'd tried to be a good neighbor to this couple who'd moved next door only two years earlier. Had invited them to cookouts they'd rarely attended. Offered a beer when he and the professor were out mowing their lawns at the same time.

Then came the pandemic and the couple's cheery, "I've been vaccinated!" stickers, which they wore under masked faces. A Black Lives Matter sign in their yard, and things grew cold between the neighbors. No cookouts, no friendly beers, or even friendly waves in the morning as they left for work.

Lord knew Dale had tried mightily to get along with his new neighbors. "Get along to go along," his mother had always said. But she was long-dead, and something rankled him about that aphorism.

The doorbell rang, and Dale stirred in his La-Z-Boy, used the remote to snap off the news channel where every word, every on-screen graphic was patriotic red, white, and blue.

His heart picked up its pace. He didn't care if the person ringing it was one of his guy's or *that* guy's. Either way, Dale was pleased to have some fun. He crossed through the narrow front hall, filled with decorative crosses and signs with sayings such as *This House is Powered by God and Love.*

Interspersed between these were pictures of his ex, Marlene, who had done the decorating, and his two daughters, all in happier times. Before the last election and the rancor that seemed to come with it. Now, none of those happy, smiling faces lived with him much less spoke with him anymore.

But that was okay. Some things were more important.

Dale saw a shadow through the front door's frosted glass, and he could make out a solitary figure holding what looked to be a clipboard. He drew the door open slowly, savoring the anticipation of whether the person would be for him or for *him.*

"Hello, good sir," said the man behind the clipboard. "How are you this excellent morning?"

"I'm fine," Dale said, looking him over slowly. The caller was in his late forties, receding hairline, a prim and fairly severe haircut with a part on the side. A narrow face, gray eyes. Medium height with a trim form. Khakis with a blue golf shirt, a small sticker on his lapel, proclaiming he was for Dale's guy.

"Well, I'm pleased to hear that Mr. ..." He glanced at his clipboard. "Mr. Henderson. I was wondering if you had committed to any one candidate in this year's presidential election yet?"

"I'm squarely for the guy on your sticker there."

The man glanced down at his chest. "I'm glad to hear that! I wasn't too sure, you know, because, even though I see some of your neighbors have signs up for the other guy, particularly your *very next-door* neighbors, I don't see anything in *your* yard. Might I ask if you're uncomfortable with your support of our guy?"

"No, no, absolutely not. I'm just trying to keep the peace and all."

"Well, maybe if I could step in and see if I could change your mind?"

"Sure thing. "Dale said, "Come right on in. Excuse the mess, if you would. Cleaning lady quit."

The canvasser laughed. "No worries, friend."

Dale led him to the living room, where he'd just been watching television.

"Have a seat," he said, motioning to the couch as he flopped into the chair. The man sat, and placed his clipboard onto the couch beside him. Dale heard Marlene's voice in his head, *Well, offer him a drink, you clod.*

Dale pulled himself back up. "Can I get you a drink? I got soda, milk, or beer if you're so inclined."

The man smiled. "Just a glass of cold water if you can spare it."

"Sure, all you want," Dale said, ducking through the adjacent door to the kitchen.

"I'm a campaign leader for this area, and my team is out today drumming up support for our candidate," the canvasser said. "I guess you know how important this election is. Everything, our entire way of life is on the table, so there's a lot to lose. To ensure that doesn't happen, we need everyone's help. That's why yard signs are an important first step."

Dale walked back into the living room and handed the man his glass of water. "Thank you," the man said, taking a long, noisy slurp.

"What about the yard signs and such?"

"Yes."

"Well, I don't want to get into a pissing contest with the neighbors. I put up a sign, they put on bumper stickers. I fly a flag, they wear T-shirts. It all starts to get a little crazy," Dale said, sitting in his La-Z-Boy.

"But it is a pissing contest, as you so eloquently put it, Mr. Henderson. All elections are pissing contests. Americans set them up to be exactly that. So, your participation, making it public, is what helps our guy win. Simple as that."

"I guess," said Dale, drumming his fingers on the nubby fabric of the recliner.

"Can we at least put you down for a yard sign? That's at least a good start," the man said.

"Well … I mean … a good start? What does that mean?"

"Just that there are levels to this. Always levels, right? Room to move up."

"I mean, I guess."

The man made a flurry of marks on his clipboard, then looked up, focused intently. "You won't regret it, Mr. Henderson," he said.

"Just call me Dale … and you are?"

"Just call me Dr. Alatryx. Here's my card. Call me anytime with problems or concerns or when you want to 'go bigger' as they say."

He handed Dale a simple white business card, just his name and a phone number in crisp, black type.

"And Dale?" he said, his fingers still on the card.

"Yes," Dale said and frowned.

"*Anytime*. Anytime at all. I'm always on call for our guy."

"Okay, sure," Dale said, tugging the card away.

"Time for me to head on out. Been a pleasure to meet a true supporter, Dale. Good day," said Dr. Alatryx, rising and heading to the front door. Dale followed, reaching around to open the door, and then stepping out onto the porch with him. It was a fine, clear spring day, sunny but not too warm, the smell of grass clippings and Bradford pear trees in the air.

"My team will be here sometime this afternoon or evening to install the sign," he said, stepping from the walkway to the sidewalk, where he turned back to Dale, a ready smile on his face.

"Now remember, *anytime*."

He moved down the block, blithely skipping the neighbor's home. Dale watched him turn the corner and disappear from view.

"Anytime, sure," he muttered, then went back inside.

÷

DALE spent the rest of the day puttering around the house, as he did most days since he'd retired and everyone had left him. At around five o'clock, he fried chicken livers in his Fry Daddy and took them into the living room to eat with a Diet Coke while watching his TV news.

After that, he flipped through channels until about 9:30, then turned it off. He went to the front door to peer out onto his yard to see if Dr. Alatryx's team had installed his sign. But there was no sign yet. Through the darkness, though, he could see the neighbor's sign for *that* guy, his name draped in patriotic colors, and suddenly it made him feel his decision to accept a yard sign from Dr. Alatryx was the right way to go.

"Fuck that sign and fuck them," he muttered, then closed and locked the front door and shuffled off to bed.

÷

IN the morning, the programmable Mr. Coffee he was so proud of himself for programming, had his coffee hot and waiting for him. He poured himself a cup, splashed some half-and-half in it. He sat at the kitchen table stacked with old newspapers and old mail he hadn't read through or thrown out just yet, groceries he hadn't put into the pantry or cupboards just yet. Sat and sipped his coffee and waited for his brain to wake and tell him what to do today.

When he'd roused enough to remember, he thought about the yard sign and whether it was there yet. He took his coffee down the hallway to the front door, stepped outside onto the porch. Another lovely spring day. But no sign in his yard, while the sun shimmered on the damn sign in his neighbor's yard.

It was early, so maybe Dr. Alatryx's team hadn't made it by yet. Still, though, it made Dale angry to see his neighbor's sign and no sign of his own. He remembered the business card he'd been given. He'd put it onto the kitchen table on top of yesterday's mail.

Dr. Alatryx had said "anytime," and this seemed as good a time as any.

÷

THE phone rang twice and was answered by a friendly woman who asked Dale to wait just a moment to connect him. Dale wondered if this was the campaign office or Dr. Alatryx's practice. The way the lady answered the phone offered no clue.

"Well, hello, Dale," boomed Dr. Alatryx's voice over the line. "And how are you this excellent morning?"

"I'm okay, doctor," Dale said. "I was wondering about that sign we'd discussed yesterday."

"Yes, the sign for *our* guy." Dr. Alatryx said. "How's it look? Wanna upgrade already?"

"Upgrade it?" Dale said. "No, no, it's not there, and I was wondering when your team was coming by to install it."

"I don't understand. My people were there yesterday evening. Are you saying you never saw it?"

"I looked before I went to bed last night," Dale said, "There was no sign."

"Oh dear," Dr. Alatryx said and tsked. "We're getting this a lot lately. People pulling up signs, taking them away, or even defacing them. Do you have any idea who might have done such a thing?"

"Not really."

"What about your neighbors? The ones with the yard sign for the other guy?"

"Nah, I don't think so. I mean, we're not on the best of terms right now, but I can't imagine they'd mess with a sign in my yard."

"You'd be surprised what all this does to some people."

"Yeah, I see it on the news sometimes. But—"

"Look, I'll send another sign over this afternoon. No worries. If they want to play this game, you might want to think of upgrading your support."

"I think, for right now, the sign will do just fine," said Dale, still wondering what he meant by *upgrading*.

"Okay, well, I'll have someone over shortly. And, Dale?"

"Yes?"

"Call me …"

"Huh? Oh yeah, *anytime*."

"Right! Have a great day!"

÷

DALE spent the day in the remains of his wife's garden, trying to see if there was anything salvageable, but there wasn't. He ate an early dinner, watched a little TV, went to bed early. He didn't bother checking if the yard sign had been installed.

In the morning, before even his coffee, he went to the front door. A few robins pecking in the lawn, but no sign. He turned, terribly angry now, and before he could close the door, he caught a glimpse, just a glimpse of the neighbors' yard sign, the other guy's name almost fluttering against its red, white, and blue background. His anger burst inside like a bottle rocket.

Dale stomped into the kitchen. found his phone and the business card and punched in Dr. Alatryx's number.

This time, though, no friendly lady answered, but Dr. Alatryx himself.

"Dale," he said, and it wasn't a question.

"How did you know …?"

"Caller ID, friend. How can I help you this beautiful morning?"

"Still no sign," Dale said through gritted teeth.

"Oh, my. That is a problem," Dr. Alatryx said. "Two signs in two days. Dale, if you don't mind me saying, your neighbors are a significant problem."

"Are you sure your team got around to it?" Dale said.

"My team is entirely dependable, as am I, Dale." The doctor's tone became low and tight.

"I didn't mean anything by it, I just—"

"Look, if your neighbors are willing to take two signs out of your yard, to ensure your voice for our guy isn't heard, who knows what they're capable of? I mean, a sign in your yard is entirely legal. Hell, it's the American way. They have a sign for *their* guy in *their* yard, don't they?"

"Yeah!"

"You've got to stand up for yourself or people like them will roll right over you."

"So, what do I do?" Dale's anger at his neighbors' transgressions seethed within him.

"Might be time to upgrade your support," Dr. Alatryx said.

"I don't know what you mean."

"You upgrade your support for our guy, and we'll take care of that problem for you."

"Are you asking me for money?"

"Assuredly not," Dr. Alatryx said, sounding offended. "It's not what *you* can offer *us*, it's what *we* can offer *you*, Dale."

Dale had no clear idea of what Dr. Alatryx meant, but those words made the hairs on the back of his neck stand up.

"My people can swing by tomorrow to put up a new sign. We're a little strapped for time. But I'll tell you what, we'll get you an upgrade, a slightly bigger sign, a yard banner. See if they want to mess with that."

"Sure, that sounds great!" Dale said, thinking about his neighbors looking out at his yard and seeing that instead of something like their puny sign.

÷

THE next morning, there *was* something in Dale's front lawn.

When he stepped onto the porch, he saw two thin metal rods had been pushed into the grass roughly five feet apart. Dale remembered Dr. Alatryx telling him his team would install an *upgrade*, a bigger sign. These two metal rods looked as if they might have supported a banner between them. But now that banner was gone.

On his neighbor's lawn, their yard sign was still intact. The sight of this incensed him. He was so worked up, he felt sweaty and his scalp itched.

He thought about marching over right now, tearing their ridiculous sign right out of their yard, but he was afraid of what else he might do … particularly if they came outside and tried to stop him.

So instead, he went back in and made a call.

÷

"THEY stole your upgrade?" Dr. Alatryx shouted into the phone. "Dale, this is serious. They're screwing with your fundamental rights as an American."

"So, what do I do?" Dale asked, Dr. Alatryx's anger stoking his own. Suddenly, it didn't matter if his neighbors even did it. At the very least, they *knew* who did it.

"Dale, as a thanks for being such a loyal supporter of our guy, it would be an honor to help you with this very serious threat to the success of our guy and, frankly, to your freedoms."

"What'll you do?" Dale said, an icy tendril creeping up his spine.

"Don't worry about that," Alatryx said. "Don't worry at all. A few men will be out this very afternoon to get your replacement banner installed. I have to say, Dale, I'm glad you're on *our* team."

"Thanks," Dale said, but the line was dead, as if Alatryx was eager to get started on whatever he had planned. Dale decided to follow his advice and not worry. He had a few errands to run and then some grocery shopping, and that would occupy the bulk of his day.

He went to bed early that evening, checking the status of the missing yard sign. Finding no resolution there, he fell asleep to the flickering glow of the TV in his room, an endless succession of talking heads blathering on about the day's fabricated controversies.

He was awakened at around 2:30 a.m. by different flashing lights, red and blue, from his front windows. He lay there, groggy and wondering if his wife was checking on whatever it was. Then, he remembered she wasn't sleeping beside him anymore. Muzzy-headed and feeling vaguely put upon, Dale rose from bed, scratched his ass through the thin pajama bottoms he wore, and went to the front door.

Outside, there were a bunch of police cars, lights ablaze, an ominously unbusy ambulance, and a crime scene van. All parked in his neighbor's driveway and clustered in front of their house. A few neighbors had gathered in the street, the police having cordoned them at a distance from the house and yard.

As Dale attempted to process this, he noticed that there was, finally, a huge banner in his front yard, stretched between the metal rods that had been there earlier. Dark blue in the lights, it featured the name of his guy in huge, white letters, with the year in red.

He turned back to the neighbor's yard. Scanning through the sea of chaos, he realized that there was no longer a sign for that guy. It was simply gone. The cold tendril that had wrapped around his spine speaking to Dr. Alatryx earlier constricted. Without volition, he stepped out onto the porch.

The moment the cool evening air touched his bare chest, a cop stepped out of the darkness, introduced himself, and asked Dale's name and whether he owned this house. Before he answered, Dale asked, "What the heck happened over there? Is everyone all right?"

"The couple next door were murdered. Horrible, bloody scene. Did you know them well?"

Dale answered a string of questions as best he could, his mind fixated on the sign missing from the neighbor's lawn.

At the end, the cop snapped his small notebook closed and asked if Dale was planning to leave town anytime soon. Dale shook his head, and the cop passed him a business card and asked him to call if he could provide any additional information. Dale assured him he would, then went inside, locked the door, and went to his bedroom. He climbed into bed, pulled the covers over him like a child reading comic books past his bedtime, and called Dr. Alatryx.

÷

"OH, come now," Alatryx said, after picking up on the first ring as if he'd been expecting the call. "It's not like they were two of *our* people. You saw their yard sign, Dale. You know what they stood for. All the stuff that's dragging us down, ruining this once great country. You admitted it yourself. They were assholes."

"But I didn't want them murdered," Dale whispered into the phone as if the police were listening through the window. "Did you do this? Jesus, they're going to think I did it, based on that huge banner in my yard."

"Who? The police? They won't bother you anymore. I guarantee that."

"How do you … I mean, who *are* you, that you can just murder people?"

"We're the team for *our* guy, Dale, and you're either on our team or not. And we want, we *need* you on our team, for our guy. Can we count on you, Dale?"

The flashing red-and-blue lights bled through the material of his blanket. He thought back to what the cop had said about the scene next door, that it'd been horrible, messy. What in god's name had Alatryx done to those poor people? And why did Dale feel as if he were to blame?

*Because*, his inner voice answered—and it spoke disturbingly in Alatryx's voice—*Because you did. And that's okay. They weren't our people. Look at all the horrid things they believed, had to believe, because of their support of that guy. Look at what their guy, and others like him, have done to your country over the last few decades. Hell, you couldn't even recognize parts of your own town, the town you've grown-up and lived in for sixty-six years. Wasn't it better to have two fewer people who supported all that nonsense? Who voted for people who made such laws? You see how valuable that upgrade has already proven to be?*

"You do, don't you, Dale?" the real Alatryx said, reading Dale's silence as easily as reading a pamphlet.

"I guess," Dale said.

"Good, then you get some sleep, and let me worry about this. And I promise you, Dale, I'm not worried. Not a bit."

"Alright."

"And Dale?"

"Yeah?"

"Be thinking of that next upgrade."

*Sure*, Dale almost answered. *Murdered neighbors was such a great upgrade*. But he simply said, "Yeah," and hung up the phone.

The funny thing was, even as he set the phone on the nightstand, he felt better about the situation. As his eyes closed and he snuggled down into the blankets, he felt as if he'd won something vital and meaningful.

÷

THE yellow crime scene tape securing the neighbor's property fluttered in the wind. But no yard sign for them anymore, while his own banner stood crisp and unflappable, defiant in the light breeze.

As Dale sipped his morning coffee standing on his front porch, a small group of people, two men and a woman, walked down the street on the opposite side from his house. He had the distinct feeling they were coming to see him. This feeling paid off when the group crossed the street, skirting the police tape and coming to his driveway.

"Good morning," said the lady. "Are you Mr. Henderson?"

"Sure am. How can I help?"

"We're with the neighborhood HOA, and we'd like to talk with you about your yard sign," said the older of the two men.

"What about it?"

"It violates the neighborhood covenants. The signage committee never approved it."

"You can't legally prevent me from putting up a political sign."

The younger man, whom Dale instantly surmised was a lawyer, stepped forward. "Legally, yes we can, though the covenants allow for standard-sized yard signs during an election. Your sign, though, is way over the size limit."

"You telling me I have to take it down?"

"At least until the committee approves it."

"And how long will that take?" Dale said.

"The committee meets once a month; the next meeting will be in May."

Dale chuckled, sipped his coffee. "I'll have to respectfully decline."

"We have the legal right, you understand, to levy fees until the sign comes into compliance. And though we don't want to, this could result in eventual foreclosure on your property, should those fines accrue without payment. Just so you understand."

"I get it. I do. But I'm not taking the sign down."

"Okay, Mr. Henderson. You'll receive a letter today spelling out your noncompliance and the per diem fine amount. Plus, what it will take to bring you back into compliance."

"You're wasting your time," Dale said, taking his cell phone out and dialing.

"Mr. Henderson, I urge you to—" said the lawyer.

"Dr. Alatryx, I have another problem."

÷

DALE awoke the next morning to the smell of something burning. He drifted through the house, checking to see if it came from somewhere inside. When he went outside, though, he was stunned.

Dale stepped out onto his lawn, feeling the dewy grass between his toes. Ash hung like a pall in the air.

His neighborhood was about four hundred homes, a sprawling suburban tract packed with people. As Dale scanned the view from his porch, at least half of the houses were gone, reduced to rubble. Some blazed, some still smoldered. Emergency service sirens blared from every direction.

People screamed over the din. But many houses were untouched, as if passed over like in the Bible story. Dale's home was one of them, while the dead neighbors' home was reduced to ash. And Dale's enormous yard banner? It was unscathed, still proudly proclaiming his support for *his* guy.

Absurdly, Dale felt a kind of pride and power surge through him, certainly out of place for what was going on around him.

Or was it?

Dale had every reason to believe the burned-out homes, the burned-out people, were not *his* people. So, what did it matter? Why should it strike him as any different than what had happened to his next-door neighbors? These were people who didn't share his values or love of country.

So, who cares what happens to them?

The next thing that hit him—and it did so unexpectedly—was he had done this. That realization caused him to drop the coffee cup to the lawn.

Okay, he didn't light the matches, but his phone call to Dr. Alatryx, done in front of the HOA people, brought this about. He picked up his cup and went back inside. When he closed the door, his cell phone began ringing. He fished it out of his pocket.

"Hello?"

"Excellent morning, isn't it, Dale?" said Dr. Alatryx. "Your sign is paying off."

"I guess you could say that."

"Of course it is. Those HOA folks will be too busy for the fore-seeable future to fuck with you about your sign. So, problem solved. Now is the perfect time to think of the next upgrade, Dale."

"Another upgrade? Just how many are there?"

"There are just a few levels left, so we should definitely move you up. What do you say?"

Dale sniffed, smelled burning wood and plastic in the air and the undercurrent of something else, almost like barbecue.

He thought of the banner in his front yard, how it must seem a massive 'fuck you' to the other guy's supporters in what remained of the neighborhood.

And he felt good about that.

"Sure," he said. "Let's upgrade."

÷

A week later, Dale was cooking out on his deck, hamburgers and hot dogs on the grill. He ignored the blare of the civil defense sirens, the whooshing whine / roar of the fighter jets overhead. None of it would touch him or his property, he was confident.

As he waited for the corn on the cob to finish, he looked up to his roof. There, on the slope of this side, was his guy's name and the year in huge letters. Moreover, at night the entire thing lit up, lending his house a Christmas-like atmosphere.

He had his trusty radio perched there on the deck railing, but his favorite sports station now only played previously taped games. This one was a Cardinals vs. Cubs game from 1988. Even so, the station broke in repeatedly with news of the conflict in his city, showing U.S. Army troops clashing with astonishingly well-equipped militia forces. They'd laid waste to much of the city center just after Dr. Alatryx had installed his latest upgrade, the signs on the roof.

He surveyed the wreckage of his own neighborhood as he cooked. Sure, there were still plenty of homes standing, plenty of people still living their lives, but so much destruction. And the images on his favorite TV news program showed it was happening all over the country.

Dale felt little more than a twinge of guilt or circumspection. Those people, *that* guy's people had brought it on themselves. You reap what you sewed, and then inherit the whirlwind. Or whatever.

Dale had a peaceful dinner out on his deck, relishing the smell of the burning meat on his grill, which almost covered the other smells hanging in the air of his neighborhood, his city.

He went to bed that night feeling damn good about his guy and his chances in this upcoming election.

The next afternoon, reclining in his La-Z-Boy, flipping through the few channels that were still on the air, the phone rang.

He looked over to where it lay on his side table.

He *knew* who it was.

He *knew* what he wanted to offer.

He ignored it. It rang several times that morning, into the afternoon, and even into the evening. But Dale didn't answer. He knew what it meant if he did, so he didn't. He felt good enough about things as they were.

The next morning, bright and early, the phone began ringing. As he dressed, Dale realized his planned trip to grocery shop had to be canceled due to the imposition of martial law. That alarmed him and pissed him off. In a pique, he grabbed the phone as it rang.

"What do *you* want?"

"Why, Dale, I only want our guy to win."

"Win what? The war or the election?"

"It's all the same now. But there is one thing, one upgrade for you to take on to ensure our guy wins it all—and you just have to say the word to get it started."

"At this point, there shouldn't be too many of *that* guy's supporters around, right?"

"You'd be surprised. Cockroaches, all of them."

It made Dale angry to think, even after all this, there would still be supporters of *that* guy. Hadn't they learned their lesson? What would it take to get rid of them once and for all?

"Okay, one last upgrade," Dale said, fuming. "How long will this take?"

Outside, the civil defense sirens increased in volume, and their pitch cycled up.

"Oh, your final upgrade is being delivered even now. I hope you enjoy it, and thanks so much for your support of our guy. Your work has ensured his victory."

Something rumbled through the foundation of his house. He dashed down the hallway to the front door. Tearing it open, he stumbled out onto the porch.

In the distance, mushrooms sprouted against the terrible blue of the sky, fire blooming within them. The first blast hit hard, sweeping Dale and his house away on a concussion of air. The second blast brought heat with it, incinerating everything in its path.

Later, as gray flakes fell from the sky, coating everything in a thick layer of what looked like fondant, one thing still stood. Dale's banner for *his* guy, firmly rooted in the remains of his front yard.

# ANDY DAVIDSON

## THE END OF THE WORLD, AFTER ALL

÷

IT was the last Saturday on Earth. My phone rang and I answered it and Cash said, "Guess what I just did."

I was in the kitchen heating SpaghettiOs with chunks of hotdog sliced into the pot. I hadn't spoken to Cash in over six years. "I don't know," I said, stirring the pot with the wooden spoon. "What did you just do?"

To someone else, Cash said, "What's your name again?"

A laugh in the background: high, sweet, musical.

"Where are you?" I said, because with Cash you never knew.

"In my mistress's bed. We're both naked. She has lovely areolas—"

I heard: "Cash!"

I glanced at the clock on the microwave. Half past three.

The pot was bubbling now.

Knuckles rapped on wood and my neighbor Elena was standing in my open door, her shape willowy against the Florida sky. She held up a six-pack, one beer already missing. In the courtyard outside, around the empty pool, a barbecue was heating up. Music played. People shuffled. I tucked the phone between my shoulder and ear and clasped my hands at Elena, who rolled her eyes and slipped through the fronds into the courtyard, where no one wore masks. It was like those dreams we used to have.

"Does Sarah know?" I dumped the SpaghettiOs from the stove into a glass bowl on the counter. Reached into an overhead cabinet for a box of Ritz Crackers. "You still employed?"

He laughed. "Is that a joke? Do you really think my transgressions are anyone's concern now that Death is on the shore, chessboard in hand?"

"Right. Reflex. Muscle memory: Cash cheats on his wife with a student; ask Cash if they've fired him yet."

"You know my dean committed suicide last week."

"Christ."

"Hanged himself in a closet. No more worries there. As for Sarah, you're better off not receiving any calls from that old number. She'll ask questions you won't want to answer. Or maybe you would, I don't know. It is the end of the world, after all."

"And the kids?"

"The Grand Inquisitor's with them. She drove up from Fort Worth. Oh, the things meine Liebe and I have been doing today—"

I heard the shifting of bodies on sheets, a girl's laughter light as sunbeams.

I put the SpaghettiOs on a TV tray and covered them with foil.

"Guess what I'm doing now," Cash said, softly.

I hung up.

÷

IT was over a decade ago, after Alice and I split back in Little Rock. We were twenty-one and fresh out of school. By the end of that first summer, without classes and friends and goals, there was nothing between us but the wrong kind of friction. Later that fall, after it was over, I enrolled in non-degree graduate courses at a state college about an hour north of the city, just to have something familiar. I got a job working at the campus bookstore, rented a duplex next door to a school bus factory. On the weekends, I drove into the Ozarks and hiked until I found some rocky vantage where I could look down on everything. My plan was simple: save money, earn a few graduate hours of transfer credit, and get out of Arkansas forever.

I met Cash in one of those Western civ survey courses offered at night. He was a graduate instructor. He wore slacks and a tie, a little magnetic name tag. He took great pleasure in the conjugation of German verbs. Before class, we'd meet in his office, a cubbyhole in the writing center's computer lab, where I wrote emails to Alice I never sent. We talked about movies, art, Faulkner. It was good for me. Or so I told myself.

Those first few months, Cash introduced me to half a dozen girls, all of them Honors College undergrads known for midnight poetry slams in a town where there was only one bar, one microphone. These girls, they were as far from Alice with her manners and habits as I could get. I admit, I never knew what to do with them. They were lithe and cat-like, wore jeans that rode low on their hips. They stood at lazy angles. I came close to necking with one, but the library elevator ride was too short. Secretly, Cash had nothing but contempt for them. "Unrestrained libido is all well and good," he'd say. "But bad writing is bad writing."

Maybe if it hadn't been for my break-up with Alice, I'd have seen him for what he was. What our friendship would ultimately become. But the heart and head were spinning, tangled up in blue.

The Honors College held secret orgies, Cash said. Their chief organizer was a nineteen-year-old lit major named Gary. He had bad teeth and was writing a novel called *Pervert*. "He read from it at the union last night," Cash told me one evening before class. We sat near the door, in case we had to bolt from boredom. A few desks over, a biker named Dennis was cramming the last chapter of Daniel Quinn's *Ishmael*. "It was junk. A sackful of dildos brought home like groceries. Horrible. The Illustrated Woman was there. Have you met her? You should meet her."

The Illustrated Woman was a bisexual art major with tattoos on her arms and thighs. "Doesn't believe in God," he assured me, "but a natural redhead."

Eventually, I did meet her. It was at some late-night, one-man performance art show in a loft in downtown Little Rock. Cash and

I drove there in his Volkswagen Rabbit. She arrived late, slipped in beside him at the end, where we sat in folding chairs among half a dozen strangers and watched an out-of-work actor recite Shakespeare, muss his hair, and beat a stool with a cane while singing "Amazing Grace." Afterward, we went across the street to a pizza parlor and ordered a pitcher of beer. I sat on one side, Cash and the Illustrated Woman—her name was Jennifer—on the other. Jennifer's tattoos were impressive, but they did not writhe or move or tell stories of souls trapped in hells of their own making. She threw her calf onto the table, rolled up the wide leg of her jeans, and revealed the Creature from the Black Lagoon. Cash bent over her leg and exclaimed, "Fascinating!"

At the end of the night, I drove the Rabbit home, grinding the gears. Cash and the Illustrated Woman whispering in the back.

Not long after, he introduced me to his wife of seven years. They had married after high school, some small town in southwest Arkansas where the skies were forever gray and the rivers rose with the rain. "You and Sarah will click," he said. "She's quiet, down to earth. I tell her all the time you and she would be perfect for one another."

We met her for lunch at the Panda Buffet. She worked as a counselor for troubled teens at one of the local high schools, had bachelor's and master's degrees in psychology. Short dark hair, small hands, sharp brown eyes. She was self-possessed and smiled often, wore her burdens with an unexpected grace. I liked her immediately. Cash sat beside her in the booth and put his arm around her, touched her hair, kissed her cheek. I sat across from them with my hands tucked under my thighs.

Near the end of the meal, Cash went back to the bar for noodles, and Sarah shifted in her seat to watch him go. She had a fine shape to her jaw and a feathering of lightest down along the ridge of her neck. "Cash wants children," she said with a sad little smile. "It's hard for me to believe sometimes. What kind of father do you think he'd make?"

I followed her gaze to the buffet, where Cash was making a joke with a dark-haired server refilling a bin of sesame chicken.

I said, "A very clever one."

Sarah laughed. "That's what I'm afraid of."

÷

THE party out in the courtyard was in full swing. Teens on skateboards washed like waves in the empty pool. Tenants milled. Lights were strung. The landlord tonged charred sausages onto folded paper plates. I brought out my offering of crackers and SpaghettiOs, set it down on a gingham-covered table for the flies, and pulled a plastic pool chair up beside Elena, who had three beers left. We reclined near a planter of agapanthus and drank and watched bumblebees hover and flit.

For a while, we managed not to talk about the news. Reports that America's cell network was failing. That JFK and Logan were shutting down. That people were turning violent in the streets of Providence. Places that were cold and far away from here.

"*Vato*," she said. "SpaghettiOs? Seriously?"

"It's like a chili."

"You see any bowls?"

I held up the red Solo cup I'd filled with ice from a cooler.

"You've been single too long."

I smiled. "Well. That's not about to change any time soon, is it."

She popped a fresh beer.

At the far end of the courtyard, a breeze blew through a rank stand of blooming Bradford pears, and the petals fell like snow.

On the ground beside Elena, a little red radio warbled in Spanish. I caught a few words: *emergencia ... pandemia ... el océano Atlántico.*

She said, "How old were you before, when we had to wear masks?"

I thought back. "Late twenties."

"You're what, now, thirty-nine?"

"Ouch. Thirty-five."

"I was fifteen. I had acne. Even after it was okay, mama had to take my masks away."

I glanced at her profile, the old pits, the shaded scars. "Whatever's in the air now," I said, "three layers of fabric and a paper filter ain't gonna stop it."

Music crackled on the little radio: a Tejano number.

"The young will live forever," Elena said. "You old people, you're fucked."

I thought of Sarah. Of Cash. I felt the sudden urge to weep.

Over by the grill, our landlord put down his tongs and cocked his head.

Elena sat up. Turned down her radio.

"Listen!" someone called out. "Do you feel it?"

We did. A rumble beneath us. The earth trembling.

Then: nothing. Silence. Stillness.

The skateboarders perched on the edge of the concrete pool like birds, heads cocked to that square of empty sky above the complex, where twilight ran in colors of vermillion and blue. In the end, it was one of them who spoke. Board clutched to his chest like a shield, he looked where the others weren't and pointed at the deep end of the pool and said, "It's cracked."

$$\div$$

IN the winter months of the pandemic, I was finishing up a master's in creative writing in Tallahassee, and Cash drove down in his Rabbit to celebrate his landing a job teaching developmental English at a community college in the ugly little town where he'd grown up. We spent the weekend drinking homemade margaritas. The Sunday morning before he left, we drove out to a wildlife refuge at land's end and sat on the beach in the chill gray light.

I asked about the Illustrated Woman. "Lasted for years," he said, "but I knew when it was over. I was drinking martinis for lunch." He admitted to faking the shakes just to get her to break it off. "I can start these things," he shrugged, "but I can never end them. I don't really understand it. But it was the right thing to do."

He wore a gray sweater, khaki cargo pants, his black frames.

Up the beach, some college kids were having a picnic on a blanket. Two frat boys and two girls. The girls wore running shorts, despite the cold, their long, tanned legs stark against the sugar-white sand. Sea oats wavering, thin and delicate.

"Anyway," he said, "Sarah's pregnant. Again."

I swallowed. Looked off to the surf, where pelicans dove and drifted.

"How far along is she?" I asked.

"Showing soon. She's been in high school too long, man. Troubled teens. What teen isn't troubled?"

"You're an asshole," I said. I said it harder than I meant to. I'd been thinking it for a while. Distance, time, perspective. So much between us.

"I used to be religious, you know," he said.

"You've mentioned it," I said.

"I'm thinking lately I hate God. I've always hated people. Now I think I hate God, too. After all, He made people."

"I don't have much feeling on the matter one way or the other."

"Liar. Did I ever tell you about Lana Poole?"

"I don't remember."

"Pentecostal preacher's daughter. Sat next to me in the back of the church when I was twelve. She was seventeen. Her father was in the pulpit hammering out the Word of God while Lana had her hand in my pants. We covered up what we were doing with a hymnal. One of those with the funny shaped notes?"

"I was a Baptist," I said. "We didn't use those hymnals."

Cash chuckled.

÷

THE day after the party, Elena and I drove into the city. We spent the morning searching for open bookstores, but almost everything was closed. Business windows were boarded up with heavy sheets of plywood. Traffic was sparse. I thought of a Bradbury story: an old man plowing his field, watching cars pass all day on the highway, as the whole world fled some cataclysm. For lunch, we found a food truck in a parking lot and sat on a bench outside Boat World and ate our empanadas. I fingered my phone in my pocket. It had occurred to me more than once since yesterday afternoon to speed dial Sarah's number. West of the Mississippi, the news now said, networks were still up. If Cash answered, which was unlikely, I would simply hang up.

A few months back, I'd sent his oldest daughter a birthday card of Fozzie Bear. I don't know why I did it. Maybe to see if they were still a family. No response, until his call the day before. Had the card prompted it? Resurrected something, out there in Arkansas?

The kid was thirteen, too old for bears, probably. The younger one—the one I'd never met—was seven. I'd only seen her in pictures Cash had sent in the mail years ago. Little notes written along the borders of Polaroids in his neat, all-caps hand: "GRACE, EASTER DRESS – 4/9/21; "BABY NELL, FIRST CHRISTMAS – 12/24/21." Whenever these came, usually at the turn of a season, I couldn't help thinking of that day in the Panda, the sad ghost of a smile on Sarah's face. Or the last day I ever saw her. The day I left Arkansas for good.

Sarah was never in the pictures.

Only Cash, holding the girls on his knees.

Their cat, licking itself on the couch beside him.

"Do you own a gun?" Elena said.

I shook my head.

She shoved the last of her empanada into her mouth. "Didn't think so," she said around it. She wadded up her food wrapper and said she'd been thinking of driving down to a marina somewhere on the coast and stealing a boat.

"But where would we go?" I said.

"What's this 'we' shit?" she said.

÷

CASH went back to Arkansas, I finished my degree, years passed. I got a full-time gig teaching at a state college in Tallahassee. He'd stopped calling, as he sometimes did, usually when going through one of his committed-family-man phases. As a first-year instructor, I got the jobs no one wanted, like sponsoring a departmental literary journal. Enter trite poems about autumn as a metaphor for death, odes to spring. Every now and then a freshman who had read his first Bukowski would submit something about shower sex or hand-jobs. Inevitably, I thought of shape-note singing and a sackful of dildos. I published these, as often as they came in, hoping I'd lose the title of "Faculty Adviser." I never did. In fact, they sent me and a handful of student editors to a writing conference in Grand Rapids.

It was not long before this that I finally sent an email to Alice. A half-hearted, lonely how-are-you. She replied. She was living in Illinois, writing for the *Tribune*. We kept emailing, and soon enough it was arranged: she would take the train up to Michigan when I came for the conference, and we'd spend a few hours together, catch up.

The conference was held at a Hilton on the river. The entire lower exhibition hall was given over to the book fair, where university and small-press publishers peddled their wares. We had our own table, stacked with back issues of our little journal no one cared to buy, not for seven bucks a pop. All day Friday, I sat at our booth and watched the table across the way, where a dark-haired woman sold copies of a journal called *Snaketongue*. Her white conference name tag was turned facedown, unreadable, her look distracted, her long fingers busily adjusting trade paperbacks on racks. She wore a black knit long-sleeve shirt, a red skirt, black hose, black leather boots. Black-framed glasses that glinted in the cavernous room's fluorescent lights. I watched her and imagined she was certain things: quiet, well read, a short story writer. I thought of what Cash had said a long time ago: *You and Sarah will click. She's quiet, down to earth …*

Saturday.

Happy hour. The lobby bar clogged with writers, the air thick with cigarette smoke, raucous with chatter. Somewhere, a piano played. I leaned against a pillar, coat over my arm, and saw her coming up the escalators from the parking deck. Her hair was shorter. She wore a white, button-up blouse that wasn't ironed and a pair of jeans snug across her hips. Circles beneath her eyes the make-up couldn't quite hide. She hugged me and her smell, the one I'd almost managed to dream away, returned: that sharp, sweet scent of shampoo, no perfume. *Perfume gives her headaches*, I remembered.

We ordered a pizza in the hotel, squeezed into a corner table in the dimly-lit restaurant. She talked about work, about movies, about the scars on her hands she gets from gardening, how every thorn finds its way beneath her skin. I looked at her, listened, but every now and then her face grew fuzzy, only to rack back into focus long enough for me to remember: *This was your idea, this was your idea.* And then the contours of her cheeks, her ears, her long neck, would blur again.

"Anyway, have you heard what's happening in the northeast?" she said.

I came back. "No, what?"

"Air force carriers," she said. "Massing a hundred miles off the coast. Reminds me of those old pictures of A-bomb tests. Seismic disturbances."

We were eating by then, soupy marinara, spongy crust.

"Do you know what's up?" I asked.

She shook her head. "People are getting sick in Massachusetts. In a little seaside village, where the local library has a first edition of *Moby Dick.* It's been quarantined."

"By the military?"

"We aren't sure. Sources are tight-lipped. People are scared."

"And you still came here, to meet me?"

Alice swallowed. Put her pizza down. Took a drink of wine. "It's why I came. I wanted to see you again, to put things right. Just in case."

"Just in case?" I said.

"I was engaged a few years back. It didn't work out. I'm fine now. I do yoga. What am I trying to say?" She drank again. "We weren't meant to be together, you and me, but we weren't the worst, either. I wanted to tell you that. Is that kind? Or cruel? I don't know. It sounds cruel, now that I say it out loud. But days are coming—"

Her phone, facedown on the table, vibrated.

She picked it up. Put it down. Her hands shook.

"When the whole universe becomes a ticking clock, a count-down, it's hard not to feel sorry for yourself," she said. "But it's even harder to make things right, you know?"

I nod, stunned.

"Soon," she said, "it may be the only reason we have to—"

Her phone, again. She flipped it over and scrolled some feed with her thumb.

I sat watching her, uncertain what to say. How to feel.

*What's wrong with her?* I thought. Then: *What's wrong with me?*

"I have to make a call," she said, and got up. "Be right back."

She disappeared into a sea of writers and starry-eyed undergraduates.

I watched her go. I watched her go and thought of a time when the two of us had loved one another, when we had been more than fumbling strangers, when whole galaxies had spun around us in a firmament of our making and there had been no lack in ourselves, no need of others to bear us away from our own abandoned shores—

Seconds later, acid swirling in the bowl of my gut, I called the waiter over, paid the check, and left the restaurant. I rode the elevator upstairs.

On the third floor, a writer whose name tag I recognized got into the elevator. Fumes on his breath, he said, "I was just down in the lobby. I have terrible gas. I farted down there and circled the room. When I came back, it was still there."

Nausea and the elevator, rising.

"I was at a party last night 'til three," the writer slurred. "The cops came and broke it up."

I swallowed. Got off on my floor. Heard the writer mumble something incoherent as the doors slid shut behind me.

In my room, I fell on my knees in front of the toilet and vomited. Emptiness emptying itself.

My phone rang as I flushed. It was Alice. I turned it off and did not turn it back on for the rest of the conference.

The next morning, I was popping Aleve in a session on character-building when I saw them: the *Snaketongue* woman from the book fair, wearing a sweater the color of television static, a blue-jean skirt, those black boots again. She sat beside a man whose square head I thought I knew, and when he turned and whispered something in her ear, I saw Cash's profile clearly. A little gray around his temples now. The woman in the sweater laughed, and her fingers found the nape of Cash's neck and stroked it, gently.

÷

"I'M driving out to see you before it all goes tits up," Cash said, on speaker.

"When?" I stood at my bedroom window, peering through the blinds into the street that ran behind the apartment complex, where a homeless man in a sports jersey and ragged pants was pinballing back and forth between two dumpsters, frothing at the mouth.

The glass in the window vibrated. The whole world had been shaking for days. A constant rumble in the ground, like big machines were turning over, somewhere deep. I wasn't sleeping anymore.

"Have you spoken to Sarah?" I asked. "Is she still with her mother?"

Silence.

A UPS truck lurched up the alley, and the homeless man staggered out in front of it. The truck struck him, sent him sprawling. Screech of tires, squeal of brakes.

"Something's happening here," I said. "I may have to call the police."

The man who got out of the truck was not wearing a uniform. Just a pair of jeans and a T-shirt. He carried a baseball bat. There were nails driven through the bat.

"It's too late now," Cash said. "She's gone."

The homeless man lay twitching on the asphalt, one ankle twisted the wrong way. His arms reached toward heaven and his hands clawed the air.

"What? Gone where?"

The truck driver spoke, then jumped back when the homeless man lurched at him. The truck driver swung the bat down, hard, into the homeless man's head. Blood splattered like paint. The driver was screaming.

"Just gone," Cash said. "Dead."

A crack in his voice.

Or my own.

Or the Earth itself.

I hung up and went away from the bedroom window and out of my apartment and straight to Elena's, three doors down. I knocked. When she opened the door, wearing gym shorts and a muscle shirt, her own phone was in hand, and there were tears in her eyes. We stood there, each prisoners of some new horror foreign to the other, and then I stepped straight into her arms, and with one hand she closed the door and with the other she held me and I held her until our trembling ceased, though the world shook on.

÷

HIS Volkswagen pulled into the complex parking lot on Thursday. The air was hot and still. The earth was quiet by then. The sun was disappearing. He emerged from the passenger's side. A girl in a yellow sundress and flip-flops got out from behind the wheel. She was young, gaunt. Her hair was unwashed. Cash and I embraced. He introduced her as Mary. She pulled me forward into a hug. "I've heard so much about you," she said. She smelled of cigarette smoke and pink bathroom soap, and beneath these a tang of body odor.

Cash insisted we go back to that same patch of beach we'd visited years before. We drove thirty miles in his Rabbit, out to the refuge. The chain-link gate was demolished. Someone had rammed it. We drove through. On our way to the beach, a massive alligator lay across the road, and we rolled to a stop. Cash got out and flapped his arms and the gator turned and hissed and Cash threw himself across the Rabbit's hood. He settled back against the windshield, drew his knees up, thumped the hood with his palm.

I drove on, around the gator. The road wound through open marsh, barren trees where eagles once nested.

Mary told the story of how they met. She was hitchhiking at a rest stop east of Tuscaloosa. The women's bathroom was bathed in blood. Cash saved her.

Wind blew palm leaves into the road. The sky was purple as far as we could see. Thunder rumbling. The water choppy, great crashing waves pounding the dunes. Sarah's name was never mentioned. Cash's daughters, I didn't ask after them. I was only thinking of Elena, the boat she wanted to steal. The gun I did not own.

We sat on the beach. There were no birds.

After a while, Cash said, "Gotta piss. You two stay here and talk about me while I'm gone."

We sat there, the shape of him still in the sand between us.

I wondered if he would be back. Or would he wander off, into the swamp, descend into some estuary where gators lurked, oblivious and hungry? Had he come all this way just to be Cash, one last time? *Best I could do on short notice,* he would say of Mary. *It's the end of the world, after all.* I thought of following him into the trees. Choking him. Drowning him.

Mary looked at me and smiled. The wind tossed a fall of hair across her face. She drew it back like a veil. Her teeth were crooked. Her expression was soft, sympathetic. It made me angry. I deserved no sympathy. I picked at a piece of seaweed. I shifted my gaze to the ocean, where the clouds roiled and arcs of pink lightning made a cage of the horizon.

She turned her foot in the sand, burrowed her unpainted toes into the beach. "He said y'all been good friends forever."

I said nothing.

She waited.

So I told her the story, the story Cash did not know.

The story of what happened before I left Arkansas for Tallahassee. Their firstborn, Grace, was three. I was spending the weekend with them and he left me with Sarah and the toddler. He said he had to go to his office, send an email to his adviser about his thesis. He was finishing up that winter. I knew what he was up to, some quick, on-campus rendezvous with the Illustrated Woman. I suppose I could have stopped him. I didn't. The front door closed behind him and Sarah was sitting at the other end of the couch, and Grace had fallen asleep on her blanket on the floor, among a stack of Little Golden Books. Between us: an empty space, still depressed with the weight of him, and the video about the cartoon dinosaur ended and we didn't move, either of us. Until I reached across and touched Sarah's hand. I saw the look on her face—brown eyes fixed on the carpet—and I knew she knew everything he had done, and she knew that I knew, too. A shaft of sunlight warmed the room. Motes swam in it. I squeezed her hand but it was like squeezing a dead fish. She jerked away and went into the bathroom and shut the door. And I sat for a time like a stranger on the border of a land I had never been to, peopled with a race whose language I did not speak.

I met Mary's eyes, large and dark, yet swimming with light.

"I'm sorry he brought you here," I said. "You seem like a better person than either of us."

She shrugged. She said, "I got nowhere else to be."

We sat in silence until Cash came trudging back. He plopped down between us. "Did you two have a nice chat?" He put his arm around Mary.

"We worked some things out," Mary said.

Up the beach, we heard a scream. A young woman was running away from a distant lighthouse, one shoe on her foot, the other in her hand. Her legs were long and tanned and she screamed and screamed and screamed.

We sat there, the three of us, upon that ultimate shore. Cash in the middle, his head on Mary's shoulder, the Gulf before us, grown black and formless as forever.

# MASON IAN BUNDSCHUH

## BROKEN SKY ROAD

÷

THEY stopped running only when the sounds of slaughter were well behind them. To hesitate was to die when the rez were hunting. They kept another silent hour of loping along the crumbled roadway and twisted slag before they paused, panting, to listen to the dripping silence, but Lehua knew that silence could lie. Sound carried strangely in the cold fog.

Hirata started to whisper something but Lehua cut him off with a harsh gesture. You had to listen.

A bird called haltingly from a crumbled building above, a rare sound, a good sign—and a sign that perhaps winter was loosening its grip. Using her spear for support Lehua clambered up a hillock of rusted metal boxes piled atop one another by an ancient flood and made herself still as stone. Sweat cooled fast in the mist. She heard the ocean where steel waves fell like icepicks on black rocks. They were out of the heart of the city, almost to the rising ridges near their camp, but there was no longer anyone for them to return to.

Hirata, standing silent in the road below, pulled crushed pine needles from a frayed nylon bag and rubbed his arms and neck to mask his scent. Lehua checked the tribe's precious gun again. Hirata pretended not to see. It was a useless, reflexive gesture, she already knew how many bullets were left. Once you ran out that was it, you were left with knife and spear. Finding more grew harder each season. Scavenging in the ruins was getting more dangerous.

"They got Will," she said finally.

Hirata made a low whistle. Will had been a good leader but he still had walked them all right into a hunting pack of rez.

*We were lambs to the slaughter*, Lehua thought as she climbed back down to the road, then wondered where that phrase had come from, and what were lambs. But she allowed the questions to evaporate. To reflect on the past was to hesitate, and to hesitate …

Hirata shifted. "We have to keep moving."

Lehua nodded, turning her hard-angled face one last time back the way they'd came as if she could see through the perpetual mist to the ruined beforetimes city. It was all the requiem that they could afford Will and the rest of their dead.

## BEFORE TIMES

"IS everyone ok?" shouted Noah over the ringing in his ears, shoving away fallen ceiling panels. "Leave it—everyone out of the building now, could be aftershocks."

His dazed office staff filed out into the humid November air, joining the growing crowd pouring out from businesses along Kalakaua Boulevard and threading among the cars stalled haphazardly across the road.

"Sounded like Big Island blew its top," said his assistant, strangely calm.

They fell in with a surge of people to the corner of the building for a clear view south. There, over the blue pacific, loomed an impossible column of fire and smoke like a gash in the sky. In silence, arcs of lightning thread through billows of ash larger than cities.

Without a signal, as if everyone thought it at once, the crowd surged back.

"No time, you can't outrun a tsunami," said Noah keeping his assistant from dashing away. "We gotta get up high now."

She pulled away from his grasp. "The building, what about aftershocks?"

The naked fear in her voice and face threatened to overwhelm him. Before he could answer, the pressure wave of the second eruption overcame them.

÷

LEHUA and Hirata kept moving away from the city, jogging with tire-soled shoes over brittle pavement. They were careful to avoid the tall stands of ugly, rasping, saw-grass. The rez didn't have great hearing, but other things in the fog did.

The gloom deepened and the mist threatened to freeze. It would be the deep dark soon and they were still on the outskirts of the city where people once lived however many forgotten generations upon generations ago. Around them the empty shells of massive incomprehensible buildings decayed—buildings that were useless for shelter, with wide foyers and walls of empty indefensible windows. Lehua had always cursed the people who'd made the cities, cursed them for their absence, for leaving only chaos and questions and questions. But asking questions of the past was hesitation, and hesitation …

A shape loomed in the mist ahead, Lehua instinctively leveled her spear, Hirata following suit a second later. A cold gust shifted the fog revealing a massive pillar of concrete and steel rearing up like the shin bone of some impossible giant. At its base, where it had fallen from the sky, lay a twisted metal box, etched with tear-streaks of rust, empty staring windows, rows of cracked plastic seats waiting for no one. People once had somehow moved around in these things, Lehua knew. Now it would only ever decay in the damp and mist along with the memory of beforetimes.

A marking on the ancient machine caught her eye as she and Hirata passed. "That symbol. It makes a sound. 'Ha'."

"Ha," he repeated.

"That," she pointed, memory a silver surfacing fish, "Makes an 'ar' and the one shaped like a tree is 'ta'."

Hirata stared in superstitious awe at the hieroglyphics printed on the rusting hulk. "How do you know?"

"There was a woman in my last group." Lehua turned away.

Hirata fell silent as he followed, remembering that Lehua had come to them when her last group had been decimated, and he too no longer had a group.

"Do you think it was my name?" Hirata looked back. "The 'hah' could be a 'hih'"

She didn't answer. Trying to answer for the people who lived in the beforetimes was impossible. Lehua walked fast now, as much to leave the messages of long-dead ghosts behind as to silence the remembered screams of Will and the rest of their companions.

$$\div$$

THE sunset was the most beautiful Noah had ever seen. They watched it from the roof of their office building. All the while, to the south, the impossible tower of burning ash spewed higher and higher as if reaching to blot out the stars.

"My cousin lives Big Island," said the doctor from suite 102b. Noah couldn't remember his name or what field he was in. "Pahoa. He sent me pictures from his backyard when they had lava coming up from the ground last year."

No one answered the unasked question, the distant column of burning smoke was the answer. But the sunset ...

They sat on the gravelly tarpaper and watched. There was nowhere to be, and no way to get there, no phones, no power—there wouldn't be for days, maybe weeks. Noah remembered hurricane Iniki when he was a kid on Kauai, remembered preparing for school in candlelight, military MREs, collecting rainwater to flush the toilet.

"I want to go home," said his assistant in a small voice.

Noah made himself sound brave again, calm, assured. It was a reflex to keep from breaking. "We'll try to get out of the city tomorrow. I bet they get H1 cleared pretty quick. We'll still have to walk ..."

They all thought of the terrible mess in the streets below left by the surging waves. Sand, trees, cars—and tangled in all, the bodies. Still, the sunset …

"We're lucky, the waves would have been bigger if Kilauea wasn't on the other side of the island." The speaker was a clerk from accounting in Noah's office, and again he couldn't recall a name. No one responded. This was at least the twentieth time the clerk had said these words after the ocean had wiped away nearly everything east of Ala Moana, driving Waikiki into the Ala Wai canal. There were gaps in the skyline but Noah couldn't remember what had been there before. How easy it was to forget the world as it was.

To the south the tower of sulfur and soot flattened out in the stratosphere above them.

"We should try to get some sleep. We can clear the lobby and see if we can find some food before heading to the highway. We'll want to start early, at first light."

But in the morning no light came.

÷

OUT of the dead city, toward the steep uplands and relative safety, Lehua and Hirata passed more pillars, wider than any tree. Relics of an inscrutable, mad people.

"I've been here before," whispered Hirata, "It's a sky path."

Lehua's eyes travelled up the alien, arrow-straight pillar. As if by magic, the fog parted—not fully, it never truly did, but it thinned enough to glimpse the delicate web of rusting rebar and crumbling concrete spanning the roof of the world. It was a thing of impossible beauty, a floating broken ribbon stretching into the mist on either side toward the next unseen tower.

"A road in the sky," she said as if the whole thing might shatter.

"Nothing they made makes sense. They were crazy."

Lehua touched the nearest pylon. Narrow rivulets of rust scrawled designs on the ancient surface.

*Did they live up there, in steel and concrete branches, carving out holes like birds, safe from things below?*

"They had so much metal," she said in awe and disgust at the decadent wastefulness of the people who'd lived beforetimes.

"Lehua, we should hurry, get to higher ground before dark."

She frowned. She shouldn't have to be reminded of the importance of getting out of the flatlands before the too-brief light disappeared. To try and understand the long-dead degenerate world was to hesitate …

She shouldered her spear.

They hadn't gone fifty paces when the rez came out of the mist.

÷

THEY picked their way toward the freeway. The ruddy darkness hanging over everything was terrible, but the bodies were worse. Noah tried his hardest not to look, not to meet their open and dead eyes. Other bands of survivors who'd taken refuge in the office buildings joined them, among them a woman carrying a child. The woman didn't speak much, and Noah suspected that she'd been homeless—though now it didn't matter much. Better to merely be homeless instead of entombed in the wreckage of their homes. The doctor from suite 102b with the cousin in Pahoa stayed with a group too injured to walk, those passing by donated food they had scavenged, promising to send responders back as soon as possible.

Noah and a dozen others continued to the H1.

"It's cold." The young mother was the first to point it out.

They all looked up to the sullen featureless sky spread over them. The warming sun was up there somewhere, invisible, remote.

Noah's assistant spoke, the pressure of sustained shock showed in her voice. "We'll need something warm if we have to spend the night in the city again."

Someone laughed. "I moved to Hawaii to get away from winters."

It was when they tried to enter the supermart that they encountered the looters.

The power was out as it was everywhere, but there was a palpable trepidation that had nothing to do with the shadows. In the dark aisles people lay drunk, empty bottles scattered around them; others staggered silently past with bulky flat-screen TVs and game systems; in the clothing section, racks had been thrown down. Still, they were able to find what they needed, layering T-shirts and sweaters. Noah was thankful that these mega chain stores automatically sent useless winter wear to Hawaii.

"Give me the tags, I'll make sure to come back and pay for this stuff later."

Someone laughed, but each of them pulled off tags and handed them to Noah.

"I need formula," announced the young mother in a dull voice. "And diapers."

Noah met the eyes of the others and in silent agreement they all went as one. The baby care aisle was gutted even more than the rest. Together they managed to scrounge up a dozen loose diapers and two cans of powdered formula that had fallen behind a shelf.

"Once we get out of the city to higher ground, we'll find plenty of people who can help," said Noah in his calm and rational voice. He hoped none of them noticed how frayed and worn it had become.

"I found this for you," said one of the men in the group to the mother, holding up a shoulder-worn baby sling. "We had one when mine were young."

Noah hurried them toward the sullen gloom of day, bundled now for the unseasonable cold.

Hard-faced men waited for them at the doors.

"Show us what you got, come on. Bags open."

Noah's group bunched up in hesitation, blinking in the dull light.

"No one stay joking, hand 'em over." Their leader was young, lean, smirking. He carried cruelty in his eyes.

Someone yanked at Noah's assistant's backpack, nearly knocking her to the ground as he tore it off. Another stepped threateningly forward even as a shoulder bag was thrown at his feet in submission.

"Hurry up, we not going take 'em all. Just our fair share."

Noah couldn't stop his indignation. "Brah, this isn't the mainland. We don't act like this in Hawaii. Remember Lahaina? Kauai?"

For one shining moment the world stopped. Under the sullen rust-colored sky, among the trickles of shell-shocked people weaving between abandoned cars and fallen telephone poles, in the distant sound of military helicopters beating the chill air, all of the world narrowed down to one soot-streaked office manager standing between predator and prey.

Noah remembered a story his uncle told of when a shark clamped down on him while surfing Hanalei. The foam and fiberglass of the surfboard were the only thing that kept the powerful jaws from shearing through his leg.

*I thought I was māke.*

*How'd you get away from it, uncle?*

His uncle held up gnarled hands and made hooks of his fingers. The eyes.

A mocking laugh broke through the memory.

"You're serious aren't you?" said the leader. "You going try guilt me with the aloha spirit?" The others laughed. "Are you stupid? Look around you."

Noah knew the moment had shifted out from under him. "We're in this together. Gotta be pono," he said lamely. "It's the difference between us and the animals."

The bullet passing his ear made a vicious zipping sound that was nearly drowned out by the flat hard crack of the handgun. Noah stood frozen for a moment as screams erupted around him. Someone grabbed his satchel and he was knocked to the ground. Forming complete thoughts was difficult, so he just let them wash over him.

The insistent wail of an infant was an anchor pulling him back to reality. The looters were gone, as were most of Noah's little band of refugees, scattered to find their own ways back home. His assistant remained, leaning over a bundle of clothes on the ground.

"Are you ok?" he asked.

She turned, face a blank tablet of stone.

It was not a bundle of clothes.

Noah crawled to her but out of ingrained professionalism he hesitated to offer a comforting embrace. Instead, he picked up the crying baby, careful to move the limp arms of the young mother. He used the sleeve of his brand-new sweater to wipe away the blood, but he only smeared it across the little scrunched up face.

One of the others who'd stayed behind pulled him up by the elbow.

"What do we do now, boss?"

Noah recognized the man from the office but couldn't recall his name. All the names were gone.

"We keep moving and stick together." Noah held the baby to his shoulder and tried to comfort it. "That's all we can do, stick together.

÷

LEHUA fired a precious bullet into the center of its mottled chest. It was pure instinct, one that had kept her alive for years. She retreated as the thing staggered away. In a moment she knew other rez, smelling the blood, would fall on it with tearing teeth.

Lehua grabbed Hirata's arm. "Up."

They climbed the nearest pylon hand over hand on the exposed rebar. Up was the only way. Ancient concrete crumbled under calloused hands, disappearing into the mist below. A small platform rooted like a fungi to the broad face of the pylon offered a place to rest. Panting and slick with sweat Lehua forced herself to breathe evenly and slowly, as she did when hunting, turning onto her belly to listen for any rez who dared to follow.

The only sounds were the harsh frustrated cries of the rez below.

"Any of them try to come up …" Hirata slipped the spear from its tether and made a stabbing gesture. "We're safe if we stay here."

"We're trapped here."

"I won't let them get us."

She knew he meant it to be comforting, and she also knew it was his way of defining his role over her as protector, especially now with the loss of the rest of the group. Since she'd joined them, Hirata had been attentive to her—not aggressive, not demanding, as others had tried in the past. Lehua knew what it meant when men noticed a woman like that. But she also knew that such complications got you killed. It was a distraction, especially out here on open ground. It meant a hesitation in the moment of choice between self and other when death sprung up to swallow your little band.

As many times before, Lehua wished she needed no one, was obligated to no one. Even Hirata depended on her now that they were in danger together. *At the very least,* Lehua thought, *let me be beneath notice*—from Hirata, from other men and their jealous women in the various groups she'd found and fled, and beneath the notice of the hunting rez. It would be so much easier to be unseen, needing nothing from anyone. No expectations laid on her. Alone.

Cold settled in as the gloaming dark deepened.

The rez were cautious enough not to climb up after them. Only one dared, hugging the pylon to make itself a smaller target as Lehua and Hirata peered down from their perch, spears raised. Lehua's strike merely raked its shoulder but Hirata's hit it square in the ravaged face and it reflexively let go. Its remaining eye bulged with animal rage and pain as it fell into the mist, the shriek cutting off abruptly.

A chorus of shouts rose from below, followed by the wet sounds of tearing.

Lehua rolled onto her back. "We can't stay here." Above them rose the rust-streaked stone tree. Metal staples had been driven into the concrete, a ladder going silently up into the cold fog.

She put her hand on the first rung, tugged it.

"Wait for me," she said. "Take the gun."

Hirata took it, saying nothing as Lehua climbed—higher, higher— to find the impossible road above them. The pillar stretched taller than any tree, Lehua found herself gripping each rung so tightly that her rough hands threatened to cramp.

*If it keeps going, maybe I'll climb out of the clouds right up to the sun.* She wondered what the sun would look like, naked in the open air. *What if the fog stretches up forever?* Her mind recoiled from the thought.

Then abruptly, the column ended. An incomplete lattice of rusting rebar stretched up another dozen feet before ending pointlessly, as if ancient workers abandoned the sky road when the change came. To her right and left she could see through the darkening fog the reaching girders of other unfinished pillars. Like all the things of the distant past, it was incomplete, disconnected, useless.

Bitter tears filled her eyes. She felt like striking something, kicking the unfeeling concrete, shrieking her rage into the mist. It was unfair. She hated them, the stupid, mad, people of before for their unfinished megaliths. Why put your hand to the knife if you have no intention of cutting?

She started back down the destinationless ladder, fighting back tears so that they might not blur her vision. There would be no escape on a magical sky road over the heads of the cruel hunters below.

÷

"DID anyone know her name?" asked Noah. The baby made noises of discontent, but no one in the group had anything to give it. They hadn't dared to try another store and Noah had led them into residential streets tucked between modern condo high rises. They were well past the reach of the tidal waves, but the shockwave from the eruption had turned the tower's windows into empty eye sockets; glass glittered on cold concrete like fallen stars.

His assistant offered to hold the baby.

They moved a little faster now, still in silence, and still pulling their jackets tighter against the chill air.

"How far off axis do you think we are?" she asked.

Noah didn't answer at first. They'd already decided that was the best explanation for the cold. Suddenly he stopped mouth agape. His assistant almost bumped into him.

Noah held out his hand. A wet, white, flake fell onto it and just as quickly melted.

"This far."

÷

"COME *down, come down.*" Croaking voices came from the swirling fog below as Lehua descended. Their voices were alien and cold, even spoken from throats shaped like a human's. *"Safe here. Come down."*

Hirata looked up at her as she stepped off the ladder. His face was sickly white. "There are five of them," he said quietly.

She lay on the metal platform beside him, looking and listening. "Maybe six."

Hirata counted the rounds in the gun and held up three fingers. Lehua cursed quietly.

"They might lose interest," said Hirata. "Wander off."

"We crawl back down as close as we dare, you shoot as many as you can at close range." Lehua lifted her spear, "And we use these."

He shook his head. "Too risky. Let's wait."

"No time." Lehua gestured to the gathering dark. She rolled on her side to face him, the heat of their bodies mingling like the waning light in the fog. "We have to do it now."

He looked at her, really looked at her, openly and fixedly. She watched his eyes travel across the lines of her face then return to her eyes. She stared back just as intently for a long moment.

"Ok," He turned back to the mist below. "Ok."

÷

"LISTEN," said his assistant. Her name was Kuulei. Noah remembered it several blocks back and vowed never to forget. "Hear that?"

In the distance drifted the heavy thup-thup of military helicopters, invisible in the deepening blood red of midday.

"We're saved!" said one of the stragglers they'd picked up after the mega store. The group surged. There were dozens of them now, and Noah didn't understand why they were willing to follow him.

"Just wait," called Noah over them. "This is good, they'll likely be checking the situation out and hopefully dropping food. But we gotta stick together and not mob them if they land." Some grumbled, Noah kept the irritation from his voice. "We're all going to get help, but let's make sure the sick and injured get taken care of first." Though Noah had deep doubts that the military was going to be of any help to them any time soon, not with everything else going on.

"And the baby," said Kuulei.

Noah pressed forward. "Come on, I'll bet they're setting up in Punchbowl. The highway is just ahead, we can see where they're going from up there."

*Everything is changed*, thought Noah, deliberately not checking to see if they followed him. *The only way we're going to survive is together.*

÷

DOWN the broad face of the great ancient pillar, clinging to exposed rebar and angled struts, carefully, carefully. The rez seemed to sense their approach, Lehua and Hirata could smell their sweetly-rotten stale sweat rising up as they moved in agitation below.

Closer, creeping, slowly, quietly, close enough to strike, close enough to leap down. Lehua slid her spear free, compulsively twisting the already tight metal spearhead—a treasure she'd scavenged several seasons past. She looked at Hirata. He raised his eyes and nodded, drawing the ancient gun.

"Sometimes I wish," she said, so low that not even Hirata would hear, as if she really only spoke to herself, "I could just shrink and shrink until I could slip into a crack."

A dark shape passed in the grayness, and another from the right.

"So small no one would ever notice me again."

The gunshots were flat, hard punctuations in the dense mist. Lehua's spear made little sound as it plunged and stabbed. A rough-made hooked pole pierced Hirata's calf, yanking him nearly from his perch. He grunted in pain but didn't cry out. Lehua's spear worked, driving into unprotected gaps in the boiled-leather cuirass. Two were down, another staggered and flailed into the dripping fog.

Lehua saw Hirata slipping, trying to control his descent as he dropped awkwardly to the ground. His blood scrawled a figure on the cement face of the pillar.

*That is your name*, she thought. *Your true name; unknowable, unspeakable, name writ in blood.*

Lehua leapt down, pulled Hirata to his feet, and propped him against the pillar.

"I'm good, I'm good. One left" he hissed gesturing with the gun as he drew his long knife with the free hand.

*I could run. Leave him. It'll hold their attention long enough.* "Maybe," she said. *The chances of getting away are better alone.*

Lehua positioned herself next to him, standing side by side, the wide pillar at their backs. She readied her spear, listening, forcing her breath to flow smooth and even.

The wet gasping moans of a dying rez made it hard to hear the others drawing near, and the hunters were certainly approaching. Carrion-breathed, misshapen by disease, eyes of empty madness. In the fog that was forever they moved, circled, cautious yet hungry, always hungry.

A shadow moved then drew back into the milky cloud.

Lehua set her feet and felt light and deadly and sad at the same time.

Hirata chuffed and growled beside her, calling to him the heart of war and fury of will to live and live and live.

"You could be small too, and we would hide where no one would ever find us."

With a guttural shout, several shapes crashed through the swirling darkness, chaotic and vicious. The mist closed in on all.

# JONATHAN LEES

## TO WHAT DO WE OWE THIS PLEASURE

÷

FOR the fourth time in his life, Arden Ray was truly scared.

The first instance he could recall arose with a storm, flashes of light ran up the corridor to his bedroom, objects he worshipped transformed into strangers and bent into bad angles.

In between the indigestion of the night skies and his own whimpering, he heard not the rap of a frail hand but the foundation rattling thud of something that might not have hands at all.

With each step through the hallway, his home became unfamiliar, unsafe. He could call for his parents, but he had no voice. It scattered in his throat, and he knew he might die before it could claw out of his mouth.

The carpet tugged with the strength of tar on his bare feet. The thud drew him closer, a homing beacon, rather than pushing him away to the corner of the closet in which he knew he should be hiding. A persistent thrum that at once terrified and excited him.

He made it to the end of the hall, and the only light shining came from the porch beyond the front door, something shapeless silhouetted in the vertical window box. And no door would hold whatever was behind it.

Ma told him there were no monsters. She said she could keep him safe.

He was eight. Old enough to know she was lying.

And even within this untrustworthy nightmare, he found the truth in the being's face that replicated in the rippled glass.

÷

ARDEN *lay stiff on something light, vibrating, floating. Hard flashes of color explode behind his closed lids. His thighs quiver, stomach contracting, and buttocks clench as the fingers dance upon his back. The freezing hollow hands flip him over, his sturdy, six-foot-two, two hundred- and fifteen-pound frame tossing around with the buoyancy of a balloon, and he cries out for Bram when its icy digits slide down his sacrum and deeper into the cleft.*

÷

THE second time Arden Ray felt fear overcome him to the point of paralysis was when he heard his mother's voice cracking in the kitchen.

She said something so familiar and although it was from the next room, her words sounded muffled. Something about something that is born again. The scent of peaches followed her muttering, sweetness mixed with a chemical sear. The back of Arden's throat filled with the tickling fuzz of peach flesh. The stench of melting plastic grew in intensity, unearthing memories of when he lit a junk store doll on fire just to watch its face burn. Its rosy, red lips still smiling even as its dumb fucking smirk fell off into clumps on the cold linoleum.

He couldn't move as the walls caught fire. His forbidden cigarette, the one she wouldn't stop nagging about, the catalyst. He winced at the blinding flames, the licks of fire rippling the air around him, dense and distorted. All that was familiar strange once again. His mother's visage became only a blackened silhouette within the inferno. She was gone, back to forever or never, wherever that was.

÷

HE *can't see his friend, but he hears him moaning. He knows the sound well. Twenty-seven years by his side, every noise Bram made felt like a favorite song.*

*The automaton's fingers stop plundering his innards for a moment and Arden takes the reprieve to try and yank his head off the platform, smashing into the steel bar across his forehead.*

*Strangers speaking and the chirping of computers reverberate off the cold slab beneath him, vibrating his raw flesh.*

*He feels something hard shove into him, and he loses consciousness. His last frame of reference is his mother's mouth opening in front of him.*

*Something about something that is born again.*

÷

THE third time, making it impossible to breathe or think, came from an admission to himself, a fear of his own creation.

There is nothing worse than making a mistake that is irreversible and the gut-yanking downward spiral that follows. He recalled how good it felt when his seed sprayed into the forbidden spaces, yet the rest of his days were spent biting nails until the beds bled, knowing he was going to pay for those momentary gratifications. He, along with the rest of Earth's population, was well-aware of this damned disease that would decimate a quarter of its citizens before the regulations started to take shape. The regulations being a rushed cocktail of online antagonism, political shaming, and squandered funding. He knew how long it took our wilted government to say something about it, their responses more artificial than the intelligence they created, the victims piling up in hospital corridors, bare distinctions between the gaunt faces of the nurses and the dying. You could smell the sweet rot of decayed flesh drifting onto the playgrounds where the approved children cluelessly danced miles away, not knowing that one good pop of clean semen is the only reason they had functioning legs and mouths that didn't contain death. Each time he wiped his mess off with a rag, sated for the moment, he could feel eyes trained on his back and he trembled, waiting for the hardened hands to drag him away. But Arden was addicted to the hunt, the danger, and the transgressions. If he was caught making the mistake, he would be sent *there* … yet no one knew what happened in there because no one ever made it out.

÷

ARDEN *fully regains consciousness as his ejaculate explodes into a tube. He remembers fragments of the vision injected into him and it has no gender. Flesh folded over flesh, his penis slipping and stiffly rebounding off walls of lubricated skin, gripping him tighter and rubbing him with a friction that caused the head of his prick to get angry and shivers of pleasure to punctuate the pain.*

*More pings and blips. Movement from above and around him. He turns and Bram is staring, the eyes of the man he spent nearly a lifetime with, the eyes of someone who never left his side, unmoving while a self-operating arm lowers a hot blade, peeling apart Bram's scrotum with the ease of a grape split by teeth. His testes are delicately extracted and placed in a polycarbonate case. Bram, the man who meant more to him than anything, faded out, the life in his eyes diminished, his body no more than a beaten leather bag spilling its contents for the greedy.*

÷

THE city burned with rain, hot hisses creating little ghosts that floated up the avenues.

Arden understood his fear would no longer be related to an incident in time, as it was a constant. He picked up the stone, smashed through the glass divider, and ran from his apartment, past the stunned faces of the neighbors he never met, understanding he had to make it to Bram before the Missionaries found him as well. The needles barely missed him, but they managed to slash his leg, gut, and arm with some form of electric razor strap. He had never run so fast in his life. Each jarring footfall pried the new wounds open and if they had a voice, they would all be screaming.

He expected to be in a world of hurt before reaching any safe zone. Like there was any safe zone anymore. Much in this new world was all illustrated to look hopeful in order to distract what was behind it all. Guess you could say the same for the old one.

Arden pissed himself. He didn't know he had to go; it just leaked out of him. He hadn't been conscious of anything going on his body since he started running. Just the overwhelming huff of his breath and the rattle in his chest. Only with momentary resting could he feel the ache of all his limbs and the pressure of his heart escaping its cage. His eyes became two throbbing sores, the burn coming from behind the sockets, and he kept touching them to ensure they hadn't detached. He had never felt a breeze behind his eyes, the wind edging the tiny globes out of his skull. Arden understood his mortality more with every step, he was no more than a tumble of guts soaked in a so-called soul, clothed in a mess of memories that added up to a hoarder's nest of emotions.

Arden found Bram at their designated meeting spot outside the abandoned diner they used to stumble to after an evening's debauchery. Heads full of rye and pockets cleaned of money, they would chew on the cheapest eats and recount their glory days as cocksmen unburdened by guilt. This night, they left quickly after arriving, not sparing an extra moment to be visible. They took to the alleys, flinching every time a spotlight swept through the bullets of rain.

He leaned on Bram's shoulder, and they held each other for a brief reprieve, worn out, hot heaving breaths on each other's neck. Clothes stuck to skin, and they stared into each other, afraid of what might be approaching fast from behind or in front of them.

No one knew exactly what caused the rotting. What they did know is that no one was exempt. People were always in panic about birthing children into a world that is twisted and immoral. Now, they were actually sanctioned against it. Wherever the disease came from, it decimated not only the flesh and the brain but the mores of society. No one could focus on anything when death greeted every house like an unwelcome relative. "A child will still play in a war zone," Arden remembered his mother saying, "it's when they become aware of emotional pain that the weight of it all will crush them."

They ran forever. Arden led Bram around the corner, their heels just missing the sweep of a spotlight. The sound of doors locking and windows crashing closed above them. There are no sirens to announce the Missionaries' presence, which made it all the more terrifying. You can just hear the humming rising in the static of rainfall. And then ...

A hiccup?

Bram stiffened against Arden, both pressed against the wall. The Missionaries don't make these noises. They're not human.

A sound erupted from the back of the alley, drenched in phlegm, another hiccup that sounded more like the gagging from your own tongue being swallowed.

They both turned quickly to the shuffling thing, dragging itself as if on two broken legs. What they thought were piles of garbage, the safety lights winking off something wet and dark, were shadows that grew limbs and eyes.

Another sickening sound, a whistling of gas released from a decaying mound of corpses.

Closer now. It's getting curious. The darkness lurched toward them, the Missionaries passing behind them, a series of shining lights and the amplified humming near enough that the vibrations tickled their feet and the illumination dared to reveal what lurked closer and—a belch released from a slit in the stomach.

They had seen blurred pictures, heard rumors of the monstrosities. It was the responsibility of every adult to talk about the unwanted, the Rotted. Even a ripe teenager could be responsible for replicating this filthy disease. Some died in birth while the living afflicted, and those not killed immediately escaped into alleys, or the sewers, licking the faces of bloated rats to calm themselves before sleep.

Arden stared down that alley into the shifting pitch, not terrified of a malformed creature or something that has teeth where its eyes should be. Something that had black tongues erupting from its chest.

Arden was afraid he would see something that wore his own face.

So he leapt back into the glare of the sweeping lights and dragged Bram with him.

÷

"CEASE."

Both nearly fell as the booming voice repeated itself, and men twice their size were yanked into the streets with blood and tears on their faces, sucked into capsule vans, and shut behind impenetrable doors. The Missionaries descended; beings composed of metals never guided by human hands into a shape that mocked. Floating above the avenue, their sweep ended as the light pivoted to illuminate the two flesh and bone men staggering away from the hiccupping shadows. It was over. Bram and Arden had made others scream before, but this night was the first they heard it come from their own mouths.

Drugged, bound, and slipped into crystal coffins sealed with codes, they didn't wake until they were processed. They approached an edifice that looked no more threatening than the average office tower, bland and faceless as the beings that ran it. They were carted past two tight doors that unfolded into interiors expanding far beyond the size the exterior led them to believe. Rooms that echoed an early 1900s saloon dusted with gun smoke was one short corridor away from a two-floor central hall house with blue tile covered in Arabic script and the scent of roasted lamb. A whale with white wings crested a cerulean sea one flight up from where rubberized silhouettes hung themselves in a crimson-walled dungeon. The salted breeze descended into a soak of rubber and blood. Bram and Arden shook their heads in disbelief, understanding this was yet another lure to get their guards down, artificial awe to cement their submission, something they had experienced daily through their phones, their art, their religion, and their news. The men brought to this kind of complex were meant to stay for quite some time, and the infected women were incinerated immediately. What they didn't know was what came next.

÷

THE *faces emerge from the light and surround him. The fear of seeing them all together makes his entire body squint. His mother's visage looks affixed by cheap glue, sliding down on one corner. The woman, whose womb took his rotted seed, crams something soft into his mouth, his eyes rolling at the sour stench of bacteria breeding in its fibers. And Bram, his best friend, arches over him and positions something large between Arden's legs. The same friend who dared them both to violate the Sanctions together for some illusory immediate delight with a woman he cared nothing for. The friend he loved most of all but was never brave enough to act on it.*

Arden knows this is not Bram or his mother or the woman who bore the offspring of a plague. Bram and Arden had heard the stories before they fatefully trapped themselves in that alley; however, they had never witnessed the transformation. The faces of everyone in their lives were the ones who had wrestled them down, beings made of algorithms visibly shifting into ones they knew of flesh. Another false attempt at comfort.

Why do they care? Arden wonders before he whispers that he is sorry. Not that they understand, or it matters. His bad decisions bear down like the thudding beast from his dream so long ago when terror and hormones soaked his pajama bottoms.

The metal fist pumps Arden until he comes, his fluids collected in a glass tube and sealed for future testing or for replication or something more nefarious, he will never know. One more figure hovers above him, the acidic stench of that dank alley flooding the room, until the expanding shadow cuts all the light from his eyes, and when he hears the hiccup, Arden turns away from the face he fears the most.

# LORA SENF

## BLIGHT

÷

HER skin showed us the truth so we locked her away.

She was born the first of October, her momma all alone save the midwife, no man to claim either of them. During that long and bloody labor (which came at the heels of a long and bone-dry summer), an inferno surrounded the village, settled deep in a valley and hemmed in by the wild as it was. Fires happen in a dry season, but this particular conflagration should have been the end—every home and shop should have burned, and the people with them. But the village was saved, and no one could say why. We weren't bad folks, but we weren't especially good or holy—no reason to think God got involved.

As the two sides of the fire met, circling and condemning us all, the child was born with a scream like a song. She came out of her momma green as spring leaves save her palms and soles, which were the fierce red-orange of embers. Her eyes were clear and smiling and the color of rain.

The fire never left the forest; the sky loosed torrents like an ocean unleashed. The village and every soul in it was spared.

The baby nursed and was calm.

The green of her skin didn't last, but enough folks saw it to know it was the truth and not the fancy of an overtired midwife and a new momma. Before the child had seen her first week, she was brought to the town square—as all babies were—to be celebrated and greeted by the folks who'd claim her as one of their own. The fact there wasn't a man standing by the momma's side wasn't unusual enough to cause much more than a bit of good-natured gossip. These things happened and we prided ourselves on being a forward-thinking people. What *did* cause some talk was the undeniable verdant shade of her little face, faded though it was by then, and those remarkable rain-colored eyes.

The most pious claimed witchcraft—the momma, the girl, or both. Some said the girl was a gift. Others, a curse. Some folks thought she predicted the future. Others, she caused it. And a few folks started a sorta-church in her name. The people left over were science-minded types who said there wasn't any connection between the baby and anything else. They said a reasonable explanation awaited discovery. Truth is, there weren't many souls who listened to those folks except themselves.

That baby refused to stay one color, and soon enough we were trying to read the signs on her skin. It caused a commotion—some folks couldn't abide the notion of a baby like that. Others became enraptured and wouldn't give the child and her momma an hour's peace.

Before the year was up, one kindly old woman tried to smother the child in her crib.

A young man with the promise of gold in his eyes tried to steal her away. He said he wanted her healthy and whole but others claimed he planned to barter his way to fortune with her pieces and parts.

Soon enough, a law was passed.

Save one day every year, not a soul saw that child but her momma, and she wasn't allowed to tell us the state of things. Only on the first of October did a small delegation hike up the valley to the house at the edge of town to pay the girl a visit. The official purpose was to wish her a happy birthday, but we all knew what they were after.

The group that went calling was a motley crew of men who had little regard for one another the rest of the year—the mayor, a pastor, a doctor, a teacher, and a Believer. They'd stay a few minutes—half an hour at most. After, each man would come back to the crowd waiting in the town square and report what he saw. Every year's crowd was bigger than the last, but the reports always went about the same.

"She's grateful to God for the gift he's given her," preached the pastor.

"She's healthy enough, if a bit thin," diagnosed the doctor.

"She's bright and capable and reads better than I do," lauded the teacher.

"We're blessed by her presence in our undeserving town," professed the Believer.

And then the mayor would share what the girl told them—rather, what her mother interpreted (the girl would speak about books she was reading and places she wished to go, but never about the stories on her arms and ankles). "We are going to have a long and difficult winter, but the snow will mean good fields come spring and a summer without fires. Our little village will grow a bit, with births and newcomers. We will prosper in the coming year."

The words were then written in a great black book and kept at city hall. The paper would report it so folks who missed the meeting would know the message. And then life would continue, the girl having done her part for the year.

That might have been the only formal visit, but there were plenty others that weren't sanctioned. A steady stream of folks crept to that little house on nights with no moon. No moon meant for easier sneaking.

They didn't make the trip to see the girl—that was a step too far even for the curious and unafraid. No, they'd take the momma gifts—mostly useful stuff in jars and baskets. Folks who didn't have a gift to give might offer labor. That little cottage was never in need of a coat of paint or shingles or a stack of firewood. Some folks said it was shameful, the momma trading on the girl's secrets like that. I say that's weak thinking—we all use our talents to get by and that's just what that little family was doing.

If the momma liked the gift well enough, she'd bring the giver to the back of the house—the side facing the forest—and leave them to stand outside the girl's dark window in a circle of lanterns so the girl could see them properly. The momma would go back in the house and look at the girl's skin. Whatever she saw there was what she reported back.

Interpreting cost extra.

And folks would slink away knowing they were going to have a baby whether they wanted to or not, or maybe a great sadness, or maybe a change of luck. Folks who couldn't afford the interpreting were left with little poems made of bits of mystery.

*Her arms are roses tonight. Thorns pierce her wrists and fingertips and climb her throat and sew her lips closed.*

Or, *She is nothing but a shadow and there are stones on her feet and clouds in her eyes.*

Or perhaps, *She's gone white, toes to hair, except a blue gem she holds on her tongue.*

Then, last spring,

*Her ankles are black and her skin's gone grey and the soles of her feet are bleeding.*

And soon after, *Her ankles are black and her skin's gone grey and the soles of her feet are bleeding.*

The girl had never given the same message twice, never mind twice in a row. It got people talking.

The third time, the momma refused to tell what she saw, but it was clear she was troubled. When pressed she nodded, *Yes, it is the same.*

She turned the next gift giver away, sending him home with his bread and cheese in hand. After that, the momma wouldn't take any more gifts and wouldn't light any more lanterns.

Soon the roof wanted repair and the painted boards peeled.

Instead of gifts, rotten milk and spoiled eggs were left at the door.

The momma started a garden out back and set traps in the woods for what small game she could catch. She made do.

÷

NOT much older than the child, I took to hiding at the edge of the forest and watching the little cottage.

At night, while the village slept, the girl played in her moon garden. I peeked from behind the trees while her momma planted it for her as a surprise and I shared the child's delight the first time she saw it—she cried with joy and I cried a little, too, but I was only a child and couldn't have told you why. Her tears were quiet, but I could tell she cried by how her body shook and by how tight her momma held her.

The child's cloak hid her hair and most of the rest of her, ever careful even in the night.

What I could see of the girl was the color of the evening sky—the very darkest indigo. Across her face and her hands and her throat a galaxy moved. All the stars and moons a boy could dream of and others no one had discovered yet. Left to her own interpretation, she was an entire universe.

I was terrified of her.

I was in love with her.

A braver child would have been her friend.

I was not that child.

She never knew me.

÷

THAT next summer, the skies were dry and the fields failed and animals starved and folks started getting sick. The science-minded among us said it all started with the barren skies and went down a logical path. Everybody else said it started with the girl and her black and bleeding feet. But how and why were questions without answers they could agree on.

The rotten milk and spoiled eggs were replaced with piles of bloody dead things and the smell attracted all the blue-black flies in the village.

There was talk it was what the girl deserved.

There was talk she would pay it back in kind.

The best solution—to protect the village and the girl, they said—was a gate and a guard and that's what they did. A fence built high with razor wire on top and six big men hired to hold the gate. They worked in shifts, two at a time for eight hours a stretch.

We thought it was enough.

It wasn't.

Crops caught blight.

Cows rotted where they fell in the pastures.

Babies died.

*Witchcraft* was whispered by more folks and with more certainty.

Soon they didn't bother whispering at all.

It became the truth because it was what people believed.

The mayor, the pastor, the doctor, the teacher, and the Believer stood in the town square. They made promises. They would get answers for the people. They would set things right in the village.

A science-minded man brought them all together, suggested reason would provide an answer.

This time, they listened.

They considered.

They demanded her hair, her blood, a bone.

The momma brought out a little sack with hair the color of nothing at all.

The momma brought out a jar half full of blood that, other than looking a little thinner than usual, seemed like regular enough blood.

The momma brought out a white cloth with a little red spot. That spot was from the bleeding end of a toe. It wasn't any bigger than a bean.

They demanded more.

The momma came out with empty hands held out to them in a plea, said she wasn't taking her daughter's finger.

The mayor said enough was enough.

But it wasn't.

÷

FOR every drop and scrap of her child the momma handed over, young folks vanished from their beds without a trace.

It started mostly with girls—girls 'round my own age—old enough to think about lives beyond their childhoods but young enough they still belonged under their parent's roofs and rules.

Georgia went first.

Then Jess.

Paula and Kellie followed, 'round about the same time.

Soon enough, boys started disappearing too, but not so many. Ian was the only one I remember.

As children vanished, the village unraveled. Otherwise peaceful folks started calling for retribution.

The mayor and the pastor and the doctor and the teacher and the Believer stood in the town square because now folks were shouting witchcraft.

"We'll get to the cause of it," promised the mayor.

"The devil has a hand in this," preached the pastor.

"She was born abnormal and grew up bent," diagnosed the doctor.

"The girl was always troublesome and wild," scolded the teacher.

"We must atone for we have angered her," whimpered the Believer.

They demanded her skin. Her heart. Her breath.

Men stood at the fence line with torches and guns and wicked blades and made sure the mother saw them all.

The momma brought out bits and bloody chunks. She was pale, shaking, and stumbled when she walked.

After a while she didn't bother to wrap them up. She brought out what might have been a piece of a lung in her bare hands and dropped the whole bloody mess at the doctor's feet. It kicked up some dust and splattered the cuffs of his pants.

She cried when she did it. The only thing she ever said was quiet, "Please let this be enough. She can't give you any more."

More young folks gone, and us killing the caged child bit by bit. How the girl stayed alive nobody could say aside from hollering sorcery from the rafters. The science-minded men had been quiet for a long while now, their reason run dry.

When a whole family disappeared, the men demanded the momma bring out what was left of the girl.

Defeated and broken and begging mercy from all the men and gods she could name, the momma brought them her child.

She carried her in her arms like an infant, staggered under her weight, and collapsed in the blood-spotted dust.

The child was sick, skin blistered and seeping and grey. She did bleed from the soles of her feet, but she bled from those open sores, too. The girl was sick, but she was whole.

There in the dirt yard of her home, the momma's housedress fell open and we saw what was underneath. Raw and ragged places where flesh was missing from her ribs and her belly and her breasts. A seeping gash sewn up with thick black thread across her side.

Women in the crowd cried out. Some with softer hearts ran to the mother and child. It was too late for the mother and too little for the girl. The momma burned with infection and bled out on the ground, holding the child to her bare chest. She cursed us as she died, "You were so busy wanting pieces of my baby you lost the souls of your own."

The child held her mother and screamed without song and soon she wore wounds to match her momma's.

With a last ragged gasp, the girl opened her eyes. For the first time we all saw her skin tell her own truth—she was the color of the night sky—the very darkest indigo. Across her face and her hands and her throat a galaxy moved. All the stars and moons a village could dream of and others no one had discovered yet. Left to her own interpretation, she was an entire universe.

She breathed out, long and slow, and then she was nothing but the color of a dead child clinging to what was left of her dead momma.

The men took turns taking no responsibility.

The mayor turned his back and said he had nothing to do with the whole lot and mess.

The pastor prayed to God to save his soul for consorting with the devil and to save the girl's soul if she had one.

The doctor opened her up after all and said she was healthy and unexceptional except that skin of hers, which seemed perfectly normal now.

The teacher started rewriting our history to fit the way things had become.

The Believer kept the toe as a relic and hid it away where no one would ever find it.

The mother and child had no proper plot, so a few of us buried them in the moon garden. No one was going to live on that land, anyway.

To my great shame, it was my only contribution to their well-being and it meant precious little to them dead.

When that girl died, didn't a damned thing change. Babies were born and a few passed too soon, crops were good or bad, storms and droughts came and went. And young folks and young families kept on disappearing.

The young ones saw more clearly than their elders. And what they saw, they couldn't abide. They didn't want any part of a town that caged and cut up a girl and her momma for no good reason at all.

The day I walked away I didn't turn back to look at my mother, fallen to her knees in our own yard. I couldn't look back at the cottage or the moon garden plot.

I wandered through the forest that still smelled of burning when the wind was right. I touched the spring green leaves and gathered red-orange berries and when it rained, the color of her eyes was all around.

# AI JIANG

## THE NEXT STATION IS—

÷

YOU hike in the middle of the night, treading beyond where the road railings fade into tall grass and farmlands. Held in your hand is not a walking stick but a crooked branch supporting your uneven gait. You're heading toward the tight-knit trees as slender as finger bones with neither skin nor flesh. Your gaze, murky white and pupilless, fix on a point those driving past cannot see.

Those who live in the town nearby say you are on a mission to see the stars, but it's impossible to see the stars through the branches and bush-like leaves clustering where the trees end. There also sits a border with guardians settled with outstretched hands and keen eyes, as well as hooked noses trained to smell difference.

No one ever told you that difference is a transgression.

And you reek of it, no matter how much detergent or softener you use or how much Febreze you spray when you can't afford the coin laundry. Just last week, you walked away from the laundromat with a half-eaten cup of instant mac and cheese, hoping the heat would keep your hands warm, but it ended up burning your fingertips. You're lactose intolerant, but the mac was cheap, and stomachache from bloat seems better than the twists of hunger.

It is not the trees where you're heading but the mountains standing behind them. But you know that when you reach, you will have to shed your clothes, the ones you wore in the city, the same ones that shielded you from slashing winds as you walked out of narrow alleys to the attack of side-eyes and sidesteps. The scent from you is not one of a lacking shower but one that tells the others you are not like them and will never be like them.

Only in the mountains can you be naked, strip your discount trousers with moth-eaten holes, strip off the single clean shirt you own, and abandon the feather vest that has long since lost its fluff, and kick off running shoes with its backward logo bought from an underground market in Chinatown in downtown Toronto that were missing its laces and with the left and right shoe mismatched. But it was a steal, so it didn't matter, and it wouldn't matter as long as you can get to the mountains.

But gurgled words throughout the trees whisper things like *never* and *nameless* bombard you until you realize that indeed you no longer remember your name.

Yet you push forth, knowing the mountains will help you remember, even if you must sacrifice your skin, flesh, bones, to feed its soils, water the grass there with your blood, offer your eyes so you can see from the top rather than have it wander, aimless, in the city, eyes glued to the cracked pavement marred with spit and paint and oil and urine and the occasional feces which you know does not belong to dogs pampered better than humans, the beloved national geese, or people whose dignities were taken from them right before their eyes and watch as passerby stomp and stomp and stomp without ever looking down to see what they had trodden.

And even if they notice, they pretend not to because that is easier than seeing the guts mashed beneath the boots, turning blue and purple in the cold of snow, the only areas where raw flesh thaws is by the occasional vents bringing heat upward from the subways. And within those tunnels, the only northern lights are the headlights of trains almost always under construction and out of service or arriving too late or too early or not at all. Sometimes that means a life saved when a rider teeters too close to the yellow-rubber-marked caution zone whether intentionally or unintentionally; sometimes it means a life caught in the northern lights, the yellow glow, the last thing someone sees before darkness.

You come across a guardian where the trees end. The mountains are so close, so so so close.

"Where is your passport?" the guardian asks with hands reached out, cupped as though begging for water. But their stoic expression bears nothing of the sort of desperation coursing through your veins. You want to vomit all the words you know, until you realize there will be none enough to satisfy the guardian.

So instead, you turn away. Take a few steps forth to make it seem as though you're about to leave. Then you turn back.

Your shoes hold together for just long enough to break through the line of guards, where graves stand out like the shadow of teeth in the night, gapping darkness on an already dark mountain like maws of your ancestors shouting with disappointment.

There is triumph when you clear the guardian, like those times you hopped over the subway payment barriers when you were short on cash, and it was more important to use the last of it on food or a quarter in the pay phone to call your family living on the other side of the mountains than on transportation, yet it was far too cold to forgo it. It is a risk, but everything has been a risk since you arrived, passport-less, nameless, homeless in more than one sense.

You just have to climb the mountain. All you have to do is climb the mountain.

But when you finally arrive at the base of the mountains, with the thudding footsteps of guardians behind you, not the same guardians as the ones who greeted you when you arrived in the city, you find you have no more energy to climb it. Within your mind echoes the same words you hear every day when you go to work as a train cleaner and when you return from it fourteen hours later to a single futon, sheet-less, with a worn hoodie as a pillow: *This is a terminal station.* Always, always you see those northern lights as the train pulls in, but never, never do you see if it could head anywhere else other than a dead end, trapped in an endless cycle of tunnels.

# SCOTT EDELMAN

## BOILING POINT

÷

ANDERSON moved through the crowded ballroom looking for somebody to talk to, but talking to nobody.

Once upon a time, he would have recognized everyone at any of the gatherings of what since he was a teenager he'd considered his clan, and in turn, would himself have been recognized by everyone, but now—and he couldn't quite pinpoint exactly when *now* had snuck up on him, it must have coalesced during a time his attention had been elsewhere—every face was unfamiliar.

Suddenly, that proverbial frog leapt into his mind, the one who lived blissfully unaware the water in which he bathed was coming to a boil until it was far too late to hop free. He'd *become* that frog! But how was that possible, here in what was the latest in a long string of hotels which had once seemed oases, here among those he'd once considered his chosen people? He'd chosen them, then they'd chosen him, and he would have thought nothing could have broken the endlessly revolving chain of that choosing. Only this weekend, continually, compulsively, he couldn't help but think—

"Who *are* all these people?"

The question vibrated so violently within, the words almost broke free and spilled out of him, but he choked them back.

Most who were packed tightly around him ignored his passage, and as for the few who turned his way as he wedged through, when their glances would catch his, their eyes, unlike those which in earlier times sparkled with recognition, clouded over ... until he moved on. Instead of the smiles and conversations his presence once caused, this night—and he had to assume it was night, for hadn't it always been night when he'd find himself in this largest of such rooms?—they kept turning away.

He'd been a Grand Master once, or had at least been acclaimed as such ages before by the ones whom those around him this year had replaced. But that was then. And that then, he could tell, was becoming ancient history, if it hadn't become so already. So what was he *now?* Of what good were the lifetime achievements which had earned him that title given by those who'd known him before, if his lifetime had led him to this?

How could it have happened, that a ballroom filled with bodies would no longer feel like family? That he'd be surrounded by strangers? For that's all they were to him now. Strangers assembled to talk to other strangers, though they didn't seem strangers to each other. He was being smothered by an entire convention of them, it seemed, so many they needed name tags. Yet what was the point of name tags when the names the tags bore were unknown to him? Unknown ... and in far too many cases, unpronounceable.

He hadn't needed name tags to attach names to faces back when he was as young as most of those around him were now. Every face had then been known to him, every name, too, as well as the stories they'd told which had brought them together. He hoped if he continued to hunt for those hidden faces, he'd find them behind all those who'd come after.

Surely there still had to be someone he knew out there, didn't there, someone he could talk to? Many someones, he hoped. Because he needed to talk, to be heard, to be acknowledged, a need far more powerful than had ever possessed him during any of the previous gatherings in this moveable reunion he'd been attending annually without a break for more than half a century.

Strangely, even though he'd only arrived at the hotel the day before, it felt as if it had been so long since he'd spoken, he might have forgotten how.

So "excuse me" he eventually said, hoping he could cut through the crowd to find the more familiar one he remembered and was (he hoped) only temporarily occluded by all the newcomers who'd forgotten him. Those two words were the extent of what he allowed to slip from his lips. Each time he spoke them, the crowd parted slowly, almost reluctantly, and then came together behind almost as if he'd never been, his wake as erased as his accomplishments appeared to be in their minds.

As he passed them by, he occasionally thought he heard his name buried in their murmuring, but no, he quickly realized it was never his name, merely the names of others he did not know and had never met, doubted he would ever meet, the names of those he believed stood on his shoulders without managing to ever climb half as high as he had.

One more push through the crowd and there was nothing before him but a blank wall, indistinguishable from the one which had been at his back before that earlier disorientation approaching dizziness had sent him searching. Had it been as long before as an hour? Or more? Perhaps. He no longer had a way of being sure.

He'd lost his watch that morning while taking a dip in the pool, or thought he had anyway, for when he returned to the chair where he'd left it, it was gone, even though he hadn't been aware of anyone else entering or leaving. But perhaps it was still back on the sink where he'd placed it before his morning shower, and he'd forgotten to return it to his wrist before leaving the room. He'd been forgetting such things more and more lately. Whatever the cause, he'd been unmoored since that loss, unmoored and timeless and uncertain as he looked for the people he was supposed to have met throughout the day. He was always arriving too late for his appointments, he supposed, discovering they'd gone on without him.

He set his shoulders to the wall, and looked back over the heads of the crowd the way he'd come, studying that far wall identical to the one which pressed so hard against him. He thought of once again plunging into the mass of people in search of someone to talk to, but after having traversed the throng multiple times already, he was exhausted, and didn't think he had one more in him. Besides, it was unlikely another crossing would make any difference.

"Excuse me," someone said to him, the two words having a totally different meaning than when he'd said them earlier during his journey. They were trying to get his attention perhaps, but the voice was unrecognizable, and he could not even tell from the whispered syllables whether the speaker was a man or a woman, so he kept looking past their shoulders in search of a familiar face, until those shoulders drooped and they went away.

Studying that back until it vanished into the crowd, he found himself remembering something a friend had once told him in a different ballroom in a different time—a friend who in a better world would still be beside him. But he was absent, absent like all the others. It seemed ironic—or so the friend had said, and only a friend would dare to say it—

Ironic that Anderson didn't care about the future.

But what Anderson had felt back then (and what he found himself feeling now as he scanned the room years later, decades later) wasn't ironic, and he'd told his friend so. Words mattered, they were the bricks with which he'd built his life, and so, no, there was no irony to be found in his feelings. What the friend claimed wasn't even true, he insisted.

For he *did* care about the future. Just not *their* future. The only future he cared about was the one he'd been promised, the future all of his friends had been promised, a future which had never come to pass, a future of gleaming towers and intergalactic kingdoms, of flying cars and instantaneous teleportation, a future where he knew everyone and everyone knew him. But now, instead, all that waited for him was this: a present where the world was not so very much different than the way it had always been, except for the fact he was all that remained of those he'd once known. He was the last of the best, and since the promise had been broken and the future held nothing better, why should he care?

It occurred to him the reason he was alone might be, could be, he hoped it was, because one by one his old friends had felt just as

he did now, and so went ahead without him.

Perhaps that meant they were all out there somewhere, waiting, and the party he was meant for continued, complete with an Anderson-sized hole in it.

His failure to find the familiar left his head pulsing, his heart pounding, and his mood demanding a drink. Hadn't he spotted a bar immediately after he'd entered the ballroom? The line then had been longer than he'd been willing to wait, so he'd abandoned it and instead begun weaving his way to the middle of the room. But he still had two tickets in his pocket provided by the event which he could turn into drinks if only he could find it again, so he stretched out a hand and steadied himself against the wall, then started inching along the outside edges of the party. Having to steady himself was something else which seemed to happen more and more often. Besides, by that point of the night, with the scrum getting denser with each passing minute, taking the long way around seemed like the only way he'd ever get anywhere.

He edged along, bracing himself against the flocked wallpaper with his left hand, and with the other making the almost imperceptible waves he'd gotten in the habit of offering up during his younger days, since back then, even if he wasn't always able to see someone he knew, he'd make the gesture just to be sure, because there always might be. But this night, he stopped, self-conscious, because now there no longer was.

Once he'd made the full circle and arrived back at the door through which he'd entered—which *had* to be the door through which he'd entered, right, as the ballroom featured only one door?—there was no bar to be found. Its absence made no sense. Where had it gone? Surely the staff would never have rolled it away so early in the evening. Had it disappeared the way his friends had, and all he needed to do to find them was follow it? He didn't know. All he knew was—he still needed that drink, and as much as he hated to pay for one when he had those free drink tickets—he hadn't had to pay for his own drink in years—it was time to hit the gift shop. Maybe he'd at least be able to grab a beer there. There was nothing here for him anyway.

He left the ballroom, left all ballrooms, understanding he had no reason ever to return. He walked the long, narrow hallway which led to the lobby, and because that is what he'd always done, peered into each meeting room he passed, his curiosity overcoming his despair. Not everyone had abandoned the day's programming yet to party, and so as he occasionally paused without entering, he was able to consider a speaker at a podium in one room, four unrecognizable panelists at the front of the next, a crowd milling in yet another, waiting to be told by a moderator to take their seats.

He once would have been at the front of such rooms, or even chosen to sit among audiences from time to time when old friends would gather to talk of better days and brighter futures, but during that night's meandering, he recognized no one. The signs by the doors, listing no names he recognized, and describing topics he barely understood, didn't call to him, didn't help him decipher the nature of this new world. So perhaps his friend had been right after all. But since he was no longer there for him to tell him so, what did it matter?

He picked up his pace, pausing before no more meeting rooms, leaving it all behind him, until eventually, inescapably, the hallway opened on the lobby. Wandering past registration as he made his way toward the gift shop, he nodded at the clerk, and wondered—even though his luggage had yet to be packed, for his clothes still hung in his closet and his toiletries remained spread out on the sink—if it was time for him to check out.

Even as that thought occurred to him, he knew he meant it in more ways than one.

But no. It was not his time yet, no matter what the blank faces in the ballroom told him, no matter that he'd yet to find someone he could talk to.

But if it wasn't time to check out, what *was* it time to do?

First, pick up that drink, and perhaps with a can in one hand and some fresh air in his lungs, he could figure it all out. As he drew closer to the gift shop, though, he could see its glass door was closed and its lights dimmed. A sign on the other side in the shape of a clock told him the cashier wouldn't return for another fifteen minutes.

He didn't think he had fifteen more minutes in him, not within a hotel like this one had become, even though he'd once thought he'd surrendered himself to such hotels forever.

The doors to the street slid open at his approach—at least *they* recognized his continued existence—and he stepped outside to a dark street which, though devoid of life save for an occasional car driving slowly past along the rain-dampened street, was no less likely to yield him the conversation he desired than the inhospitable ballroom he'd escaped. What should have been an oasis inside was now nothing but a desert.

Immediately to the right of the entrance, he dropped to a wooden bench, grimacing not from its hardness, but rather when he realized how close he'd sat to a butt-filled ashtray, another reminder of how much the walls of the world had closed in. Tobacco had never been his drug of choice, but still, he shook his head and thought back longingly to the old days when no one ever needed to slip out of a hotel to grab a cigarette, which meant the faces of his friends had never been obscured by strangers, only a constant cloud of smoke. Some would call that progress, but not Anderson, who found the presence of the former not quite as dangerous as the latter.

He tilted his head and tried to see the stars. None were visible, but that was to be expected, the latest comfort kept hidden from him. For of course the lights surrounding him were far too bright. He suspected they always would be.

He heard the whoosh of the doors beside him sliding open, and before he could turn his head to see who'd joined him, an octagonal plastic token was tossed into his lap. It was red with a large gold number printed on one side, and a hole above that number so, he assumed, it could be hung from a hook. He turned it over in his fingers, uncertain what he was meant to do with it, then looked up, seeing one of those who'd replaced the ones he'd loved. He did not know the young man, and knew he never would.

"Fun time's over," the stranger said. "I wish I could stay longer, but it's time for me to head home."

And then Anderson understood.

He turned and noted the nearby stanchion on which a small metal box had been mounted. He almost laughed, but held it back, for it would have been an ugly laugh. Not only hadn't he been recognized as one of them—he never would be again, he knew—but instead had been mistaken for …

"I'm not—" he began to protest.

Then stopped.

He rose, suddenly feeling lighter than he had in years, and flipped the token in the air, then let it land in his palm with the number facing down. He walked over to swing open the door of the box, which revealed rows of key rings on hooks. He ran his fingers along them until he found the one hanging beneath the number which matched the token he'd been given.

He wrapped his fist tight around the fob, at the same time nodding at the stranger, feeling he was nodding not just at him, but at all the strangers who'd slowly, inexorably, invaded his life. Then he turned his back on the man and walked through the roped off area of the parking lot clicking with a thumb until he heard a honking and saw flashing lights.

He climbed into the stranger's car, started the engine, and adjusted the seat—but not bothering to adjust the rearview mirror, for he would never again need to look behind—then drove away from the hotel off into the night which he finally understood had always been waiting.

# EUGEN BACON

## CINDERS IN YOUR HAIR

÷

IT'S safer in your head than it is in nameless streets where rivers bleed and children don't stand quiet in kitty pajama tops, blandly gazing and sucking their thumbs. You know a world where it all goes to shit, hemorrhaging waters starved for language. You know it because it is your world.

You know the baggage someone carries when their maw strings herself up? That's the kind of rough you got on you, and Maw ain't even dead. It's the fantasy you walk around with in your head, thinking what if, for just a second, it were true? What if she kilt herself, not gave you away?

> You speak to a moment
> but no love unfolds—
> bullets tear your heart
> in a cosmos history
> … must judge?

It's safer in your head, strewn with fragments of rainbow and metaphors of cats stretched out and languid, but their blue and amber eyes stare at you and they're all guilt-ridden. Colors a little too close in your mind share their opinions, and they're more contentious about the weather than about real people listening to how ice groans, or watching online videos of everyone turned to turtles dancing on TikTok.

No one cares if it's a metaphor or AI.

What sort of parents give you away? What thoughts linger long and hard to tell them it's okay to let you go? They waited enough for you to remember the shape of her breast, the curl of her fingers around your palm. The smell of cocoa butter on her touch soft as a petal. The hue of her skin is a distant memory now—how dark or light, but you know the comfort of its nearness and the feel it gave.

You remember the timbre of Paw's voice, the orange and white light dancing in his eyes as he read you a bedtime story about the monkey and the crocodile. His sound is a fade now, the audio and texture of it. But you remember the angle of his face, how he turned it just so in your direction, his long, immaculate fingers holding your favorite book.

Do your real paw and maw in turn remember, you ask yourself over and over?

Have they carried in their heads your first smile? Folk say a newborn smiles. Do they recollect your first reach and grab of her hair, your first crawl to him, your first pull levered on his leg or her chair to stand by yourself, your cry as they walked away? You wonder if they replaced you with another much-loved child, or if, instead, mourned the loss of you with laden hearts full of unforgiveness and hatred of each other.

You say this to the psychologist because the new ones call you a problem child, as you wrestle from day to week with over-friendly grown-ups who would rather pretend what you're not, what they're not. You don't tell the shrink that you want your real maw to suffer greatly. To kill herself in a death that will take forever and a day. And, when she does, you want to be there so you can touch her body, feel her convulsions, hear the distress in each breath as she wrestles for air, an aggressive struggle for oxygen that ain't coming. You imagine pink froth secreting from her nostrils, her mouth, her eyes, how she falls unconscious, and her muscles go rigid. Eight-to-ten minutes— that's how long it takes to die when you string yourself—are not enough for the agony you want her to feel.

You carry this fantasy in your head, and it makes it a little tolerable to smile the first time at each new mother. They're all different.

But they have one thing in common: meddle. Loud or quiet, it's still meddling for your loyalty, your affection, as they squeeze you into hugs that feel all wrong.

The places the system puts you, they're all decent. Like the house on Gladwin Avenue with two courtyards, back and front, one deck and a solar-heated swimming pool you sometimes dipped your toes into. That was alright. The six-bedroomed apartment in a leafy suburb walking distance to the beach was chill too. Even the townhouse on Norma Street, all roomy and alfresco extensions, your own bedroom self-contained and with two walk-in closets. Nothing wrong with it. Then why did they find you that first night out in the courtyard, all alone, mist in your breath? Shivering under bright, bright stars, and clutching yourself? You don't know if it was anything to do with the new mom, a wiry little thing that swayed with the breeze, her eye ticking all the time, nothing chill or alfresco launching itself in your head each time she showed.

"You're causing some headaches," the shrink now says.

Are the headaches because you don't greet each new one with fireworks and shrieks of glee? Is it because the words "maw," "paw" are a universe away,

> no secret or legacy to decode,
> too far and too alien
> for your tongue
> to shape
> them?

If there are hugs you want, it's not *theirs*. You are a ghoul haunting their waking dreams, everyone's waking dreams, the real and fake moms and dads.

It's safer in your head but is the emptiness you feel a plague of years? Cats are no help, and some homes do have cats, but there's something reassuring about whorls of cerise, indigo, cantaloupe, magenta, ruby, ginger and scarlet vacillating in your head. No surety of what they'll uncover, and you'll never know what they think.

"What you have is rapid intensification," the shrink says.

÷

THE new mom shows you to your room that's all that space, mirrors everywhere. It has a valet stand, a showroom cabinet with a chalice lamp—a huge globe in the gold that priests use at the altar to drink wine turned into Jesus's blood. You take in the Paris king bed of "brushed oak"—she says. Snooze clap lights that fade to a quixotic hue. "See if you like it," she says.

"I like it," you say.

"There are more rooms. You can try another one if you want."

"I don't. Want."

The new dad has a walking cane. He doesn't creep up on you, silent, like the other dads, spooking you, or sometimes themselves. With this one, you can hear the clop, step, clop, step miles before he shows into a room. His grin is real, full of marshmallow heart. You can never tell what keeps his thinking this happy all the bloody time. What you can tell is he can never lift you if you fall. Perhaps his disposition is because he's listening to the shrink:

"It's all about growing the resilient child," she says. "Safeguarding against depression."

Your new parents join the Self-Esteem Movement, slogans for psychological immunization all over the fridge:

*Each day is new. Your journey begins today.*

As if you want to be in an eternal odyssey. The wind at night sounds like a passel of mating possums.

What those parents are trying to do, using all those slogans, is called para-fiction: filling in the gaps. Gaps, fiction or not, they too give you away, and you ought to be happy, but something the window saw …

÷

THE curious window unhinged from the pane of a house that bordered a thicket in the east and a hillock that fell to a gruff coast in the west. She shadowed a child clasping a candyman's hand, walking away into the woods. Torn jeans and a T-shirt, his jacket the color of

dirty trees. Her charcoal curls, his gray mop, the girl cast a backward glance, her tiny palm wrapped in his fist until the jaw of the thicket swallowed them. When the candyman shape-shifted to become the bogeyman, the bewildered window floundered back to her house, locked herself to an infinity of crystal tears.

That's what the window saw.

÷

WHY do you keep dreaming this dream? It's not that you fear the country or the ice or the bogeyman. You're not afraid of other humans, but theirs ain't a chronicle of love, but of need, sometimes war. Their "help" makes them, not you, feel better, and your disquiet churns to a silent rage. New moms and dads you don't need make you a blot, then a gruel, sickly green and oozy, a melt of bile … Trapped in the time capsule of a hound's howl.

And, each time, you step back into your body, wonder who will find you, when?

Still the system asks you to trust those with whom you live. Those you should … love? Your counsel is a nacreous moon that topples from the sky in a spectral cartwheel, splashes into a black river as the town sleeps. Unclued to

> the silence of your cell
> where night is
> the fingerprint
> of a
> curse.
> This another window saw.

It's safer in your head because you're not supposed to ache for unbroken promises. Nothing startles like the silence of a fulfilled wish. The night's fingerprint wipes out every curse. You need no father, or a mother. Not even a cousin or a friend. Just yourself.

So why do you topple with the hound's howl, cartwheel from the sky over and over to no chronicle of recycled love? You cell your trust, as in verb it, action it. Put black hearts inside a breakfast bowl that you gobble.

÷

THEY thought a boarding school in rural country would settle the fiends, grow you out into a happy, resilient child. No one asked what you wanted.

It's safer in your head between summer and fall when you satisfy a temporary wanting by turning a whole school into cinders. Is it the malevolence of bitch girls and the opulence ranking of their homes? The spite of segregating boys and the falsity of their supremacy? Perhaps it's your flawed childhood.

It's safer in your head as books shriek and collapse from library shelves, and the science lab draws a last breath before it swoons. Is it the unsolvable maze of the geography lesson and its roots and shoots, creative sustainability: tuning to animals, people and the environment?

A school is just a school—when its teachers and students burn, it is nothing. You wash petrol off your hands as the blaze crisps bodies like overcooked turkeys unscripted in a barbecue.

Is it to satisfy a curiosity about how human bodies blister and scorch? The scientist at heart tossed a match and held dominion over life and death as orange flames roared in your eyes.

÷

NOW you're pre-teen, and you need the kettle on. With lemons that are not for eating or drinking, just lemons that will recycle allegories of novels, poems, broken promises. Nothing aches like lost trust nobody wants, left there for you to find. Can't nobody—anybody?— give you a biscuit to dunk in your tea?

When lights blink out with a reminder that you're halfway to hell, no one is a boat or a crossing. Nothing makes a safe landfall. Your world is a crow's nest on an iceberg that irks or bores, even as it turns your fingertips blue.

At first, you attribute the cramps to the tightness of your jeans. Then you realize it's your period. But what collapses onto your sanitary pad is a little creature, then another, little flies with eyes and human ears, bleeding and bleeding out of you until the horror of blood begets a beast.

That's what the new window saw.

You can't sleep. The house is full of other people's dreams.

You spend the night at a supermarket, then a 7-Eleven, a petrol station, even a 24-hour chemist called No Indication Handbook. There's no obligation to buy, you know this. Why can't you drop in and browse, pass an hour or two without needing to get a solid sell in with a wallet and a credit card? The old man at the chemist doesn't look like he's carrying a gun. He's welcoming—not so much the young'uns you sometimes get. Looks like he might offer you a swig from treasures under his desk. He's a fixture and a detail. An all-nighter who knows how to survive his funereal world. His face is a casket and an urn. Your tears well up as he winks at you.

You haven't thought of your childhood all these years, kept no notes back to front, alive and pulsing, about how it was before they tossed you away. This old man is a name whose letters you don't recognize, but the sequence beats with the alphabet of your heart. In another life, you might recognize him—is he your grandpaw?

You are kindred. You need a tape measure in your hands to touch on him so you can remember him. "Old, old, man. Who are you?"

It calms you, filling the time like this, making a phantom of you instead of other people's dreams. You're at ease with suspicious staff in all those places, ease because what they show you is their true selves, no pretense.

A young man with a fresh stubble and blond dreads at a night shop peers at you over individually-wrapped cakes of soap—coconut, lime, rosemary, mango ... A new adult—you can tell she's new to this kind of thing—at another shop catches your eye between necks of bottled olive oil ... A mother—she is a mother with little ones she cares about, everything about her face says this, the way her fingers fondle disposable nappies—locks gaze with you around stacks of umbrellas ...

To each, you smile and say, "I'm leaving." They have no obligation to respond, but he, she, they touch their ear, chin, slowly nod,
eyes still startled, and you know

> they'll count everything,
> even all those tins of
> two-fer cat food.
> 'Cos something the window saw …
> The window saw.

It's safer in your head because the circus is a paradise where
everything happens. You long for self-burial where nothing happens,
and reason will not die. Sorrow is a spell, generative and misun-
derstood. Sorrow is inefficient to communicate when nobody is
listening for it, no one noticing each attempt of escape to escape.
Sorrow is a few things ready to go, no reward tiers to trouble anyone.
It's just a dirge that waltzes over a fence, pirouettes to the black wail,
now you're the dirge, starlight on your face, ice in your core

> forever and a day,
> an enveloping pain
> swollen with
> melodies.

It's safer in your head because you can't decide what to do with
your heart: so you layer it on a garland of new flowers on a grave that's
not your maw's. You take no notice of the walking dead that seek
memory or touch, that will tear you from the wish you left behind.

÷

THE new dad has a white beard and a polo shirt, black corduroys and
a dance in his stride reclaiming his youth. He's a DIY-er, though the
mansion on St George's Court doesn't need much do-it-yourselfing.

"Look," he says and shows you his shed. Polished tools smelling
untouched: a power drill. Shears. Gloves. Spades. A Remington steel

axe. As if you'll love him for his showcase.

Your new mom has a tee tossed over an apron, paint on her face in a color you'll later get to know as "amaranth." She's an artist. She looks flustered, but shows you her art. "I'm an action painter," she explains. Splash. Drip. Smear. You take in her canvases, splashes, drips and smudges on them as abstract as the pieces of your life—just more flamboyant in mustards, yellows and peachy pinks. Twilights, corals and spices. Cardinals, springs, chartreuses, fuchsias, ochres, chalices, sonics and sands. Pairings, too …

The light in your room is too bleached, too jolly. Your bed is too featherdown, when all you need is solidity—something, someone to hold your frame.

New mom shrugs, says, "Guess you don't know it's the right place until you try it."

"It's the right place," you say firmly, more to convince yourself than her. "*It is* the rightest place."

"Do you know how to cook?" she asks.

It's safer in your head where you feel blue, what a classic. There's a party in your head. Could take a few scalps, decimate them with the raging fire that grows bigger inside a city of mirrors, all eyes shimmering, reflecting their full thoughts of you.

What's an unlikely future, how might it look like?

It's safer in your head, the thing too noxious to exist outside your skull, and you—the antichrist best lodged in your cranium than in the real world. You mull about castles and clouds, tattoos and teardrops. You're desperate to pull off your fighter gloves, at war with the universe. You want to have a good rest, set up right. Find the difference between skin and bone, soul and spirit. Your heart is already well protected, no one can ever near it. No one to steal it, stab it, hack at it.

Hack, hack.

You sit in the basement of the house in St George's Court, feet facing your new maw who's asleep. Her head is splashed, dripped, smeared with an egg yolk of brain. Not the gray-white kind you might find pickled in a lab or at the back of a butcher's store. Your new paw will find you like this, your eyes telling him that it's the end of days, apocalyptic in the cathedral of flames you wish to consume everyone who turned a bland eye, then looked away, who prayed to a host of numerology to determine your fate, as if it could. Your eyes and every cursed demon in you will dare him to love you or leave you.

His is a no-choice. If he leaves you, he could well have held the axe with its gleaming tip of Remington steel. If he loves you, he's lighting the licking fire that ought to soften the light inside the igloo of your heart that stretches and yawns, races out in the fields without socks or sandwiches, going nowhere fast toward high ground.

It doesn't matter whether he'll survive this. You will survive this.

You'll try not to talk about it, glove your feelings in all circumstances. Pummel them into shape, just not to pulp. So they sprout, stem and twine into palms, thorn trees, baobabs … Arching, looping and whirling in turquoise, chartreuse and fuchsia with action sentiment tending toward a testament that ought to be a DIY script.

And, maybe, a person who puts oil, salt and pepper on shit, and it comes out tasting like carbonara casseroled in truffles, like bloody hell, WTF, yeah that one … maybe they might sway fate, get a peek at that heart, though it'll leave you feeling like a goose.

You remember the old chemist at No Indication Handbook. How he was open-hearted, despite his funereal face. How he reimbursed your toddlerhood when you hadn't thought of it in all these years—the way it was before the letting go. How you couldn't have reasonably anticipated that you'd come to terms with unavoidable skulls, and that shape, touch, scent, hue and timbre from your babyhood would come rushing back. And you wept because only weeping could mutate you all the way from the attic to the basement, and draw a line on the love letters of what, until now, you didn't know exactly as grief.

> And each specter at the window will know
> that it's safer in your head
> where candy blood flows
> and cinnamon cinders
> scorch your
> hair.

# CLAY McLEOD CHAPMAN

## THE NOCTURNAL GARDENER

÷

Inspired by "What You Discover When You Garden at Night" by Daryln Brewer Hoffstot, *The New York Times*, August 8, 2023

THE heat index peaked at a hundred and two today. The temperature's been teetering in the mid-nineties all week. Any hope of gardening under the pummeling sun has completely wilted. Lord knows I've tried. I've slathered myself up with enough sunscreen that I resemble a shriveled spirit. I've donned a floppy hat that leaves me looking like an elderly mushroom cap. I've even set up an umbrella and hunkered under its shade, clinging to what little cool air I can.

Nothing works.

I'm sweating five minutes into pruning. The fatigue seeps into my system, no matter how hydrated I am. The humidity simply slips under my skin. Soaks into my bones. I'm waterlogged by the time I settle in, baking before I even begin, all groggy after a few snips.

It's the dizzy spells I worry over.

My husband has banned me from our backyard if the

thermometer ever climbs over ninety degrees. That's most days now. He has good reason to worry. Last month, Walter found me passed out in my raised tomato bed, crushing the poor seedlings I'd just planted. He rushed out of our house, straining to make it to me in time. What he must've thought in those fleeting moments, I can only imagine … It took all his strength to lift me up, my face flecked in topsoil.

*Agatha … Agatha, wake up. Speak to me.*

*Where am I?* How confused I must have sounded, so utterly disoriented. I couldn't focus on his features. Who he even was. The upset expression on this stranger's face terrified me.

*Agatha, it's me … It's Walter.*

*What's going on?*

*You took a spill.*

He struggled to slip my arm over his shoulder and heft me onto my feet.

*My seedlings.*

Cherry tomatoes had burst beneath my body, their tender stems snapped.

*We'll worry over those later. Let's get you inside. That's it, one foot in front of the other.*

Now I'm under close watch. Walter won't admit it, but I feel his gaze upon my back whenever I step outside. He lingers by our bedroom window now, keeping a close eye on me.

It's not as comforting as one might think, gardening when there are prying eyes on you. Always surveying every last snip. Waiting for those first signs of heatstroke. Ready to pounce.

He's right. As much as I loathe to admit it, setting foot outside during the day is far too untenable. I can't spend time in my own garden. What do I have left? All of our children have grown, with families of their own. It's merely me and Walter now. There are but few pleasures left in this life. Cultivation is my most prized pastime, but the sun has taken that away from me.

So I've switched. The moon is my ally

I have become a nocturnal gardener.

Instead of battling against that ungodly heat, I'll wait out the sun. I'm no longer under that wrathful eye in the sky. The second ol' sol sinks into the horizon, I'll sneak into the yard.

I've found I prefer tending to my vegetables in the dark. The humidity holds no domain during the dead of night, when the air is cool against my skin. There's far less sweat.

It's taken some getting used to. For my eyes, mainly. The backyard has closed in on itself. What before was a lush length of lawn, enveloped by my beds, is now all wrapped in shadows.

The world—my world—has changed. Constricted itself. But I don't mind. Dare I say I prefer it—this myopic landscape—reduced to this tiny patch of land. My soil. My garden.

Dusk would suffice, but midnight feels much more special. Walter thinks I've lost my mind, waking up in the middle of the night and crawling out of bed to prune in peace.

*Why on earth would anyone choose to do that to themselves? It can't be healthy.*

*I've slept my whole life. Who needs more?*

*Your husband, for one.*

*I've spent enough time with my eyes closed. I want to make the most of what time I have left.*

I didn't have the heart to tell Walter his snoring keeps me up most nights. Rather than simply lay there in bed, wide awake, on my back, staring up at the ceiling and cataloging the cornucopia of aches and pains my body has to offer ... I'll go outside. To my other bed.

Walter gifted me a headlamp. *So you can see what the hell you're doing,* he said.

I slipped it on over my head, flipping the switch. *How do I look?*

Walter winced, shielding his eyes. *Like a miner.*

I liked that. I imagined digging deep into my raised beds, tunneling further into the earth, winnowing through its darkest chasms, my path illuminated with my new headlamp.

*I love it,* I said, kissing him on the cheek. *Thank you.*

*When will I ever see you now?* He sounded mournful, as if he was losing me. Letting go.

*You can always come with me, you know? Stay up. Step out. It'd be an adventure.*

*It's after my bedtime, I'm afraid. I'll wait for you in bed.*

I'll kiss him on the forehead when I climb back in, trying not to wake him when I slip under the covers. He lets me sleep in. I won't wake until late in the morning. Sometimes lunch. Walter won't complain—not anymore—when I remind him who's reaping the reward of my nocturnal gardening. Where does he think his cucumber sandwiches come from? The grocer?

We're simply on different schedules. Here we are, in the twilight of our lives. Two ships, as they say, right here in our own bed. Walter has the day, while I have the night.

I have earned this stillness. There's no one out here. No honking cars or barking dogs or drifting conversations from nearby neighbors. No deliveries. No phone calls. No nothing.

It's simply me and my night garden.

We've reached that point in the season where I must bid farewell to my lettuce. The time for tomatoes is upon us. Beans and zucchinis.

I'm tackling my planters tonight. Tying off the stems with twine to keep them upright.

There is no world beyond what is in front of me, what the beam from my headlamp catches. It helps me focus. The world melts away. Not from heat, but my consciousness. I've never been so meditative before.

I'm turning over a new leaf, you might say.

Even my arthritis relents in the dark. I do believe the drop in temperature eases the inflammation in my wrists. There's far less swelling in my joints than there was in the sun. I can spend hours outside and never wince once when I snip. Walter gifted me a pair of pruning shears for our fiftieth. Two years ago. *It has a soft cushion grip*, he said fondly. *For your hands.*

I didn't have the heart to tell him I could barely squeeze these sheers shut. I had to hide the fact that I wasn't strong enough to use them back then.

Not anymore. Not now. Not in the night.

The sheers are still new. Sharp. The stainless steel blades glisten under my lamplight, a set of crescent moons, a pair of lunar twins, slicing through the darkness.

It's simple to lose track of time. I do nearly every night. It's only when the sun peeks over the horizon that I realize it's dawn. Time to pack up my tools. Head back to bed. To Walter.

*It's so lonely*, he told me over lunch. A tomato salad. *I never see you anymore.*

*Have you thought about picking up a hobby?*

*A little late for that, don't you think? Old dogs, new tricks?*

*It's never too late. I've done it, haven't I?*

*Are these our lives? Our routine from here on out? Are you ever coming back to bed?*

*This is who I am, dear. I'm sorry. I am a creature of the night now.*

It takes time for my eyes to adjust to the dark. Even then, I slip on my reading glasses. They work best, I find. Everything within my worldview is right here in my gloved hands.

There are no birds at night. Only insects. The cicadas saw away. Crickets chirrup.

I chirrup with them, humming right along.

This is our song.

Wait.

There's that sensation again. The feeling of eyes on my back, as if someone were leering over my neck.

Walter must have woken. Is he in our bedroom window?

I turn toward our house.

No, the window is empty. The lights remain off. Our bedroom is nothing but a blackened chasm. So where is this feeling coming from? If it's not the sun, if it's not my husband, then …

Who's staring at me?

I keep still. Let the night settle over me. This distilled stillness. A palpable blackness.

I wait. Listen.

Your body adjusts to the night. Your eyes. Your ears. Your skin. You never realize how many sensations the day takes away, while at night, the darkness sharpens them. I've become something completely different. Something new.

I'm not alone. I can sense it. I know this because my vegetables tremble.

There. Just a few feet away from me. On the other side of the raised bed. Peering from behind my planters, I find a pair of sapphire eyes. At first, I think they are cherry tomatoes.

But then they blink.

Something is here. Hiding in my garden. With me.

My breath catches. My grip tightens around my pruning shears. *Hello?*

It could be a raccoon. A possum, perhaps. A deer? It's not out of the realm of possibility that a black bear could have crept into our backyard, finding solace in my garden.

*Is someone there?* I have absolutely no idea why I call out to it, whatever it may be.

What if it answers?

My eyes aren't what they used to be. Even the beam from my headlamp can't reach that far. Whatever is hiding on the other side of my planters is blurred, a green shadow.

It shifts. The tomato vines writhe.

*Who are you?*

*The night is not yours.* Its voice sounds congested, lips brimming with topsoil. *The night is mine. Go back to your—*

Before I second guess myself, my pruning shears spring up from my lap and—

*Splk!*

—I bury the blades into the soft contours of its chest. It lets out a cry of surprise.

How often have I heard him hurt himself over the years?

*Walter?*

He slips out from behind my planters, collapsing face-first, crushing my tomatoes. I grab hold of his shoulders and lift, but he's too heavy. I can't do it. Can't carry him. The best I can do is flip him over so he's staring up at the stars. His anniversary gift to me is still embedded in his chest, spring-locked handles reaching out for me. Already I can hear the blood flooding his lungs. Every labored breath is wetter than the last.

*Walter, oh Walter.* He's bleeding into my raised bed, his blood black in the night.

*I just wanted you ... to come back ...*

*Back? Back where?*

*To bed.*

*I ... I can't do it. I'm sorry, I don't think I can carry you inside. I'm not strong enough.*

*That's all right, he says. Just tuck me in here.*

We've traded one bed for another. We share this one now. Walter is with me whenever I garden. We're always together. I only go inside when the sun comes out. I sleep during the day, waiting for dusk. When it's dark enough, I'll crawl outside and begin cultivating that night's crop.

Beans. Zucchinis. Cherry tomatoes. Bell peppers. Kale.

Over fifty years went into this harvest. More blood, sweat, and tears than most marriages. Now we lie in bed together blanketed under the stars, the cool air on our skin.

# ERIC LaROCCA

## YOU ARE THE EMPTINESS IN
## EVERY ROOM YOU OCCUPY

÷

I find myself carting your withered corpse to the market every Saturday morning, your shrunken, bloodless arms dangling from the side of the carriage and bouncing lazily while I pull you along. I now keep precise time by the arrival of Saturday morning, realizing you're due to be loaded into the wagon and then shrouded with the white linen I've scrubbed the night before and perfumed with jasmine to keep away some of the smell. You didn't offer much of an odor when we first began, your body practically as scentless as a newborn calf. But now there's an awful stench that lingers in the air whenever I'm in your presence for too long. It's not that I oppose the smell; however, some of the others at the market have told me that such a scent might be off-putting to a potential buyer, a prospective client.

The wagon creaks as I drag you toward town and I remember that I must fix one of the wheels when we return from the market later this afternoon. Of course, that's only to say if we return together. Perhaps today will be the day that I finally part with you. Yes, perhaps today will be the day when I accept a generous offer from one of the many gentlemen who approach us at the market. There's one gentleman in particular who has been circling

us the last few Saturdays and seems eager to make the sale. Although I admire his enthusiasm, I can't tell whether or not I wish to offer him your body. It's not that I expect he'll perform lewd and lascivious acts as some of the other market patrons have been accused. Rather, it's that I fancy him somewhat and I don't know whether or not I want to saddle him with the task of caring for and tending to you. After all, you must admit that you carry a greater sense of responsibility given your impressive size and, most importantly, the reputation you had cultivated before your untimely demise. Surely, I know he'll respect your corpse and tend to you the same way that I've nurtured your body all these years since you first passed. However, do I dare burden him with such an excruciating responsibility? Of course, there are many fine rewards to keeping your loved one above ground after they pass—the respect from the community, the abundance of companionship. However, there are just as many burdens when tending to a body that has been hastily preserved for alternative means.

I'm sure you've heard the gruesome tales of families—usually forced by the male head of the household—who keep their loved ones from burial only to subject their lifeless bodies to such depravity, such perversity. It's revolting to think trust can be broken after one finally perishes. You expect your loved ones to care for you, to make the decisions you would want most of all. Naturally, there are times when I've wondered, *Did you want me to keep your body from a proper burial?* Of course, our options were limited, considering the fact that money was tight when you finally passed after the cancer robbed so much from you. It was a pity we never had the opportunity to discuss what you wanted exactly—what you might have preferred. I spend hours upon hours talking to your corpse in the kitchen when I've propped you in one of the folding chairs, telling you that this was the only option, promising you that I'll do everything I can to tend to your needs. *I know we haven't talked about this, but I'm sure it's what you would have wanted,* I tell you. You don't react. How could you? But sometimes I pretend that you thank me, that you offer a slight nod of appreciation and whisper with a heavy sigh that you're proud of your only daughter, that I've managed to salvage the remnants of a God-awful travesty.

However, it's a horrible ruse. You probably think ill of me, especially lately since I've been carting your corpse to the market with every intention of selling you to the highest bidder. I can't pretend to think that you're not cross with me. Of course, I had every intention to care for you and keep you home as long as I'm alive. But so much of your body has already begun to disintegrate and because of this, you don't resemble the mother I once cared for, the mother I once loved so deeply. Even though I used to arrange your body in the bed beside me while I slept, I've taken to abandoning your corpse in the living room and draping you with a sheet so I'm not startled by your hideous, hate-filled expression when I use the toilet late at night.

It's not that I'm afraid of you. It's not that I want to rid myself of you and seek happiness in other things. But you know full well that we could use the money. Or rather, I could use the money. Still, it seems so unnecessarily cruel to pass you over to some stranger and hope they care for you as well as I've cared for you for the past two years. Yes, two years. It's been that long. You probably didn't realize, especially since I don't like to remind you of how long your body has been a vacant vessel. I hesitate to refer to you as something so callous, but there's a part of me that knows your corpse is hollow. There's no warmth residing inside you. The spirit that once found home in you has unquestionably flitted away in search of another body to serve as its host.

Still, there's a reason why I cart your body to the market every Saturday morning and then return to our little apartment every Saturday afternoon, cursing myself for not taking one of the offers I've received. I simply cannot bear to part with you. No matter how much I may want to cast you off and accept the payment for the toil and torment I've endured the past two years.

I shouldn't have said that. It's not that I feel as though I've suffered or have been burdened unnecessarily by you. There's obviously a reason I can't bear to sell you at the market. A reason that goes well beyond the judgment" I might receive from our neighbors and loved ones. After all, we know full well that it's frowned upon to panhandle your dead for the sake of payment. Still, that doesn't prevent the countless familiar faces I see wandering toward the village center on Saturday morning, carting their little red wagons stuffed with lifeless bodies of all ages.

Part of me thinks I should turn around and return home. *Yes, I shouldn't go through with this*, I think to myself. How could I possibly hand you over to some random stranger for money that probably won't even be enough to cover the rent? Perhaps if I received more of a worthwhile incentive to sell you off, I could be persuaded. But even then, it would be nearly unbearable to part with you. You know how much I love you, how much I adore you. There are certain things in this world that define you, and consequently you are nothing, stripped, barren without them.

Still, the young gentleman who approaches me at the market's entrance seems to make every point that I will persevere without you.

"How much?" he asks again.

When he smiles, I notice how one of his teeth has been engraved with a pair of initials—JP. I wonder if the initials belong to him and I'm about to ask, but he pushes himself forward so that I'm cornered in a most uncomfortable way.

"How much?" he repeats.

But I immediately wave him off, shaking my head. "I shouldn't have come here. This was a mistake."

He maneuvers himself in front of me once more and I curse my slowness, my inability to avoid him. He's persistent. I'll give him that.

"I think the two of us can come to an arrangement that benefits the both of us," he tells me. "I've seen you every weekend. You turn down offer after offer. Clearly, you're a discerning merchant."

I swallow, the muscles in my throat flexing. "Yes ... I can't sell to just anyone ..."

He seems to admire my discernment, my shrewdness.

"What if I proposed an arrangement that made it so you wouldn't have to part with your loved one?" he asks me.

Naturally, I'm curious. After all, I can't tell you how many times I've backed out of a meaningful deal because I found myself unable to part with your corpse.

I don't resist him as much anymore. In fact, I sense myself softening in his presence.

"I'm afraid I don't have the means to take care of the asset in question in the first place," he confesses to me. "So, I would never dream of making you part with the body."

"Oh—?"

"Do you know my most miserable grievance?" he asks me.

I think for a moment, a little uncomfortable by the question.

"An abundance of money with no real use for it," he says. Then laughs.

I don't know whether or not I should join him, if the line was intended to be as humorous as he's made it out to be.

"I'd be happy to pay your rent for the foreseeable future," he says. "In exchange for private visitations with the asset."

At first, I shake my head in disbelief and wonder if I've heard him correctly or if I've invented something in my foolish propensity to daydream mid-conversation. Can that be true? Does he intend to pay my rent in exchange for private meetings with your corpse? It seems too outlandish to be factual.

"You mean—?"

"I'll gladly pay what you need to live," he tells me. "All I ask is that I'm able to visit with the asset when I so choose. Privately, of course. No chaperones."

There's a part of me that curls a little bit, distrustful, when he mentions how he'd prefer to visit without a supervisor. After all, what exactly does he plan to do alone with you? Naturally, I've heard stories of charlatans doing unspeakable things to preserved bodies for the sake of pleasure. But the young man seems so well-coiffed, so neatly manicured and fashionable to be a filthy pervert. Yes, perhaps it's foolish to base an entire assessment on the young thing's appearance. However, he looks so remarkably dignified. More to the point, he looks like someone so out of place at this open-air market on a hot summer day, so decidedly uncomfortable in this lair of degradation and shame. Yes, there's a distinct sense of shamefulness lingering in the air. It's a horrible secret passed among all those who bring their dead loved ones to be auctioned off, to be sold to perfect strangers.

"That's all you want?" I ask him. "Private meetings with—my mother?"

He nods gently. "If you're willing to part with her for a few hours of the day."

Naturally, I'm willing to part with you for a few hours. It feels cruel to confess, but there's a part of me that yearns for a moment when I'm without you—when I'm on my own and responsible for nothing, for no one.

÷

HE arrives at the apartment late one Thursday afternoon after I've made a cup of tea on the stovetop. I offer him a cup, but he waves me off and tells me that tea has never agreed with his digestion. He says his stomach is far too sensitive. I can't pretend to understand his reasoning, so I show him into the parlor where I've arranged your corpse to receive him. It's amusing to think that you're still receiving and entertaining guests as you so often did while you were alive.

Once I deliver him to you, he regards me as if I were a nuisance, as if I were an unwelcome visitor in my own home. I squint at him with a look that I hope he can comprehend. He had seemed so charismatic, so charming at the market when I last saw him several days ago. I had trusted him. Now he seems more thoughtful, more deliberate in his every action, as if his movements were being observed by an invisible jury.

"Shall I leave the door open?" I ask, skirting toward the small room's only exit.

"Please close it, won't you?" he asks, glancing at your body.

While I pass him, I notice he's brought a large black bag made of genuine leather. At least it looks like genuine leather. It's the kind of satchel physicians used to carry around when they made house calls late at night. Naturally, I think it's curious he brought something so large, with such a terribly ornate gold buckle. But I certainly can't ask him why he's arrived with it. I'm too shy, too cautious to upset him until he pays me.

I drift out of the parlor and close the door behind me. The latch fastens as though I were sealing the two of them inside an ancient tomb. I can't imagine he'll find a sense of companionship in your presence. After all, I've sat many times in rooms with your corpse. Every room you occupy is lonely when you're in it. Even though I talk to you and pretend you have the ability to respond, the moments are hollow. I am so numb when I'm around you sometimes, as though I were put on this earth to exist in total isolation, to dwell uncomfortably in the stillness of empty rooms.

It was foolish to think I'd feel somewhat freer knowing you were being tended to by a perfect stranger. It was unreasonable to imagine I'd feel joyful and content, knowing you were occupied and were no longer my permanent responsibility.

Even though I had planned a few activities to enjoy while the young man met with you, I find myself incapable of doing anything but sitting at the kitchen table and staring at the empty counter. It's amusing to think how I'm alone once more. I'm with your corpse and I'm alone. I'm by myself and I'm alone. I'll never be surrounded with people or friends or loved ones. Instead, I'll only exist in liminal spaces. I'll dwell in dimly lit waiting areas, forever on the precipice of something else—impossible to actually and finally arrive.

An hour or so passes.

My attention remains fixed on the door to the parlor. The silence has been so unnerving, chilling almost.

Finally, the door opens, and the young man emerges from the room with his leather bag in tow. He looks a little flushed, his bowtie kinked in a knot and his glasses crooked until he fixes the way they rest on the tip of his nose.

"You're leaving?" I ask him.

He smiles, flashing those tiny initials engraved on his tooth.

"I told you I wouldn't be long," he tells me.

He's about to head out, but I stammer, unsure how to bring up the prospect of payment. He owes me, after all. Even though I was too shy to question him about the curiousness of the leather bag, I'm not too restrained to ask about the money. The money is the whole reason I agreed to this unusual proposal. He recognizes my frustration and excuses himself, setting the bag on the floor. He fishes inside his coat pocket and pulls out a checkbook. He writes with a black fountain pen and then passes the check to me.

"That should be enough to cover this month, correct?" he asks.

I look at the number he's written on the line. It's almost too much money. But I won't question him this time. After all, he owes me for the peculiarity of his presence. He's been especially odd during this initial visit.

I nod in agreement.

He swipes his bag from the ground and makes his way to the door.

"I'll be back next week," he assures me.

But before I can respond and ask him about the day or time, he's already out the door and hastening down the hallway toward the elevator. I can't call after him, so I shut the door to my apartment and fasten the lock shut.

I stand in the kitchen for a moment, gazing at the numbers on the check he's written for me. It feels so underhanded to take his money, to whore you out in such a grim fashion. *But what else was I to do?* Besides, he merely wanted to visit with you. I know for certain he wouldn't have done anything to undermine your integrity. It would be too cruel of an act for him to undertake.

I pin the check to the refrigerator with a magnet and make my way into the parlor where I find your body exactly where I had left you. You're slumped in the armchair, your head listing to one side and your mouth hanging open like an untreated wound. I'm about to rest my hand on your thigh and say something to comfort you when I notice something peculiar about your mouth, like it's been forced open, as though your jaws were pried open for an extensive period of time for some kind of unnatural labor.

I lean in closer, squinting, and it's then I make a horrible realization. There are a pair of letters etched into one of your remaining teeth. The letters are dark—black as ink almost—and they spell the initials "JP." It looks as though the letters have been carved into your tooth with some kind of sharp chiseling instrument, your mouth left to hang open and your lips forcibly curled as if hopeful I might notice the grotesque disfigurement.

I nearly retch at the discovery. *How could he do this to you? How could he mark you as if you were nothing more than cattle?* Part of me wonders what other horrible things he did to your body while you were incapable of objecting, but I'm frightened I'll upset myself too much if I truly consider the vile, obscene scenarios that could have happened in this little room.

It feels cruel to admit, but you're tainted now. You no longer belong to me the way a mother's dead body should belong to her child. You've been marked by another. You've been soiled, branded by a perfect stranger. A notch in his belt. An addition to his ever-growing collection. Yes, that's exactly what you are. You are nothing more than an asset to be collected, to be savored, experienced, and then cast aside.

I expect he has no intention of returning to this place. He's already gotten what he was truly after. He wanted to mark you, to carve himself into your body and make you his—a gem to be included in his grotesque collection of lifeless victims. I have no doubt he did other things to your body while he was alone in the room with you. I'm too scared to look beneath your clothing, to see how you've been stretched in certain private places—how well-worn you've been because of his lust, his insatiable and perverted longing.

I should have never attempted to keep you here. I should have accepted one of those many offers and sold you at auction. At least I wouldn't be burdened with the knowledge of what's finally happened to you—how you've been so pitilessly violated, how you've been forever desecrated. You are damaged goods. An unfit thing to be loved. I cannot and will never love you again.

You don't belong to me anymore.

You belong to him.

I curl myself into the armchair beside you, your withered arm snapping like a stick of kindling when I absentmindedly apply some of my weight there. I could break apart more pieces of you, scatter them around the apartment and revel in the sanctity of your presence one last time. But I'm too forlorn now. Everything's been ruined. As though I've been defiled, too.

I pull my knees tight against my chest and sink into the leather armchair beside you. I will not eat, will not sleep, will not relieve myself ever again. I'll die in this place right next to you. I can only

hope the young man will return next week and break into the apartment to finish what he started. Yes, perhaps he'll crawl in through
one of the windows and make his way into the parlor where he'll
find the two of us—expired, languishing there in the summer heat.
Perhaps he'll open his leather satchel and draw out one of those
instruments, prying my lips open and exposing my teeth like a show
horse so he can finally go about his labor, so that he can carve those
same initials into my teeth.

The two of us will then belong to him—his dead girls for show,
his loveliest collectibles.

I know we haven't talked about this, but I'm sure it's what you
would have wanted.

# GARY A. BRAUNBECK

## BEGGIN FOR THREAD

÷

"... Stooped down and out you got
me beggin for thread
to sew this hole up that you
ripped in my head ..."
– Banks

IT was a little around Oh-God-O'clock in the morning
when a man in a wheelchair rolled up to the Traveling
Memorial Wall set up near the Cedar Hill Veterans Park.
Rain from earlier in the evening had fizzled out, leaving
in its wake dozens of misty tendrils that rose from the
sun-heated granite surface of the wall, spiraling upward,
spirit-arms reaching toward the sky as if much larger
ghost-hands were supposed to reach down and take hold
of them. The man in the wheelchair almost smiled at the
stretching mist; it reminded him so much of what dawn
was like in-country, waking behind the thick bushes close
to the rice paddies, watching as the sunrise warmed away
the rain from the night before (it seemed like it was always
raining), creating mist-figures that swirled up and around,
joining hands, dancing to greet the day, only to be scattered

moments later by these large, magnificent white birds that erupted from nearby trees. The man in the wheelchair never knew what those birds were called, and when he tried describing them to those who *might* know, he found the vocabulary available to him was at best insufficient and at worst uncomfortably pitiable; maybe there were some things in this world that just shouldn't be diminished by words that awkwardly and futilely attempt to convey their mysterious grandeur. He at least had that memory to bring him some measure of consolation late at night, alone in an unkempt three-room apartment in a shabby neighborhood where tired and used-up, spirit-broken people wandered from street to street, corner to corner, looking for work, looking for some spare change, looking for liquor or drugs or day-old bread in Dumpsters behind restaurants where they would never be able to afford a meal.

"Jolly old bastard, aren't you?" he said, shaking his head at the cheerlessness of his thoughts, his mood, his life. "It's a bit late to start navel-gazing now, Schopenhauer, 'cause you know what you find when you navel-gaze? Belly-button lint. You may quote me on that." He gripped the wheels and began rolling closer to the black granite wall with its seemingly countless names carved in pleasant Optima typeface, arranged in neat, orderly, mathematically precise rows, offering a visually aesthetic balance to its record of deaths, of the POWs and the MIAs. He had to hand it to Maya Lin; it was a powerful work of art, not even close to being the "black gash of shame" some politicians had christened it.

From the downtown square less than a quarter mile away came the sound of a speeding car, windows down, blasting music. The man in the wheelchair cocked his head to better hear the music, tilting his boonie hat to the side to expose his good ear, and was surprised to hear Grand Funk Railroad's "I'm Your Captain" rolling and pounding through the night. That song had meant a lot to the guys in his platoon, gathering when they could around small battery-operated radios with sad-ass, taped-together antennas fully extended, hoping that the disc jockey at the AFVN station out of Quáng Tri that day would play it. Wasn't a man one of them who didn't want to be closer to home, just not in pieces, not in a bag, not as the grotesque punchline to Country Joe's "I-Feel-Like-I'm-a-Fix-in'-To-Die Rag." Although some of the guys from his platoon who'd bought the farm probably did get a sick laugh out of that. Afterward. Maybe. All things considered. Stay tuned; request hour is coming up.

He rolled to where the sidewalk began to slope downward, releasing his grip on the wheels and just letting the chair glide along on its own for a few seconds, just long enough for him to slip one fingerless-gloved hand inside his flak jacket and remove the Smith & Wesson M1917 pistol from its homemade shoulder holster. Using his other hand to grip the nearest wheel, he counted *seven* and brought the chair to a skidding halt, the tires squeaking only slightly against the wet concrete as the chair slid about a foot to the right, stopping completely in front of the section he'd visited four times now—not counting tonight—since the wall arrived. It was a lovely section, it was; clean, not-so well-lighted ... and the only area where no security cameras could get nibby.

"Yeah, okay, not the most graceful entrance, I admit it, but not bad as these things god—anyone disagree?"

The wall issued no opposing opinions. He took that as a good sign. Reaching out, he placed the fingertips of his left hand against its surface. "Amazes me how you can hold heat like this. A guy I know from my Vets group who visited your Namesake in D.C.—that is to say the Real McCoy—told me that even in December, even when it was in the twenties, you still hold the heat of the sun. Good. Good for you." Pulling his hand away, he readjusted his boonie hat and sat back in the chair, reading the names, remembering the faces of the ones he knew and imagining those of the men he'd never met. "I'm guessing the rain and humidity doesn't bother you too much now, does it? You're lucky. This weather plays hell with my body from nose to toes—what toes I can still feel. Goddamn diabetes, guys. Lost my right leg to it last year, and the left one's so weak I can hardly—ah, fuck it. I won't bore you with specific complaints—it'd take less time to tell you about what *doesn't* hurt these days." He stared at his reflection in the background of the names like some freeze-frame shot under the closing credits of a film, and the expression on the mug looking back at him seemed to be wondering why, when he faced himself like this, the man he saw looked nothing like the one he remembered. *Navel-gazing again, stop it, it don't mean nothin'.*

"It don't mean nothin', guys. I don't think it ever did."

The wall remained silent, listening, all at attention.

"I appreciate your listening. I won't take up too much of your time, I promise. God knows we've all got places to do, things to go ..." He caught sight of the numerous objects and envelopes that spread out at the base of the wall, extending in both directions for as far as his less-than-spectacular eyes could make out; photos, teddy bears, flowers, watches and pieces of jewelry, notes scribbled on popsicle sticks pushed between the small openings between each section, a child's tricycle, a few old Aurora monster models (Godzilla, Frankenstein, and the Gill Man, a worthy triple feature if ever there was one), a half-deflated beach ball, homemade cookies in sealed plastic bags, keepsakes that meant the world to whomever had brought the offering to the wall but meant nothing to those whose name the ornaments, charms, letters, notes, or knick-knacks was meant to honor; still, it was a way for the survivors to remind themselves that at least they remembered these honored dead, these lost prisoners of war, these always-to-be missing in action whose faces would never again be seen, whose voices would never again be heard, whose non-being left a series of holes in the places they used to inhabit, holes that now hummed with their absence.

"I see the mighty Cedar Hill, O-Hi-O Parks Department is as on the ball as ever. In D.C. people would throw shit-fits if their offerings were left out in the rain like this. I heard that in D.C. they collect these ... well, *offerings* is the best word I can come up—or is maybe *tributes* the better word? Yeah, I think tributes is the better word. *'Offerings'* sounds like something out of a horror movie about Satan-worshiping cults, something you'd expect to see Boris Karloff or Peter Cushing be in."

He thought about the tributes he'd brought along tonight, the you-should-pardon-the-expression treasures he would offer in sacrifice to the wall as an apology for having survived, and wondered if anyone would bother trying to guess their significance, let alone who had left them, and why. Tongues would be a-waggin', that's for sure.

He pulled a folded envelope from the breast pocket of his jacket. The thing was old and discolored, bearing a handwritten address that appeared to have been scribbled by some child who'd just learned how to write, and it was easy to see that it had been crumpled into a wad several times before being retrieved and smoothed flat again.

The man in the wheelchair stared at the letter never sent and so never read by the intended addressee. He was expecting to feel some kind of regret but there was only an annoying, onerous sort of wearisome resignation, the sense that he was leaving a small piece of a weight that someone else would have to deal with moving because he'd pulled into Nazareth, feeling half past dead, and needed someone to take the load off and (and) (and) put it right on themselves.

He realized that he was humming that particular song by The Band. He stopped it at once. He pulled one of his useless medals from his hat and tossed it as best he could so it might land facing out from the wall. Which it did.

"That's an apology for my being thoughtless, humming that song like I did. You guys died taking the load off and putting it on yourselves.

"Y'know, I was only four years old when the Geneva Conference divided Vietnam. Ho Chi Minh took the north and Bao Dai took the south. What the hell did I care that the French had gotten their asses handed to them at Dien Bien Phu? It had nothing to do with me, with *any* of us. We were *kids*, for chrissakes! How were we supposed to know that nine years later Operation Rolling Thunder would pretty much seal our futures? Kids. Every last one of us. Now look at me—I'm *way* on the wrong side of sixty and you guys, on this wall, you never got the chance to grow old, to lose your way, to start coming down with Christ-only-knows-what diseases because it turns out we got sprayed with some of our own shit and nobody bothered to tell us or knew how it might affect us down the line.

"Sorry, fellahs, don't mean to get all sentimental on you, not on such an illustrious occasion." He waved the M1917 pistol frontways and then sideways, just once, just enough to get the point across. No need to show off.

He read through the names again, searching through his rapidly-fading memories of these men—these *kids*, he reminded himself. Most of them didn't make it to their twenty-first birthday. For more years now than he cared to admit, sometimes—usually late at night when the pain woke him and he was waiting for the Dilaudid pills to kick in—he wondered if he should envy them … but that felt a little too close to self-pity, and *that* left a bad taste in his mouth.

"Hey, do any of you remember a couple of nights before that fustercluck at Phu Bai, we were all sitting around the radio shootin' the shit, and one of you—I don't remember which genius it was who came up with the idea—but somebody decided to get abso-tively-posilutely all ra-ra sis-boom-ba John Wayne-patriotic and suggested we have everyone say *what* they were fighting for—and "Getting my ass out in one piece" was not an acceptable response. Yeah, we laughed it off because we were tired and scared and knew damn well only half of us—if that—would be coming back, so nobody really gave an honest answer. A couple of us didn't answer at all. But lo and behold—a few nights ago, my answer came to me.

"This thing I want to tell you about, it started around three-o'clock in the a.m. I got woke up by this loud argument coming from the apartments across the parking lot. A man and a woman were screaming at each other, cursing, saying the foulest, cruelest things you could imagine. I sat up in bed, pulled back the curtain, and looked to make certain that the man wasn't beating on her. I can't stomach bastards who beat on women or children.

"The woman, you see, she was throwing a couple of suitcases into the backseat of an old used car that looked like it was only held together by spit and wishes—and I wasn't too sure about the spit. Looked like something that shoulda been sitting on a front lawn on cinder blocks. Those are the only types of vehicles that people who live around me can afford, you see. Hell, you oughta get a load of the heap *I* drive with its rusted doors. Seems like every time I start it up, some other mystery part drops out of it …" He pulled a silver flask from one of his pockets and—laying the pistol in his lap for a moment—unscrewed the cap and took several deep swallows.

"So I just quit driving the thing and sold it for scrap metal. The mechanical gizmos that helped me to drive and use the pedals helped raise the asking price, though. Now I just use the paratransit buses that run all night on the weekends. Now … shit. What was I talking about? Oh, yeah—the foul-mouthed packing woman and her husband.

"But here's the thing: standing between the woman by the car and the man in the doorway of the apartment was this little girl, no older than three or four, who was crying and screaming at the two of them to stop, please, please stop. Neither of them paid her any attention. Finally, when both of them stopped to catch their breath, the little girl walked toward the woman and said—and I remember these words exactly: 'Please stay, Mommy. I am sorry for whatever I did and I promise that I will get better. I promise. I will be better. I love you. Please do not go.' Her voice was a hoarse, spirit-broken thing, and what tore my heart out the most, even more than the sound of her fear and confusion and pain, was that this little child, this girl of no more than four or five, didn't *use contractions*. It was like she wanted to make sure that her mother clearly understood the intent of her words. Maybe she learned to use formal words from watching *Sesame Street* or something and was hoping it would surprise both her parents, y'know—make 'em *proud*. Maybe she'd been using too many contractions in her speech and it annoyed one or both of them, and this was her way of showing them that she could do better." He shook his head. "It made fuck-all difference. Both her parents screamed at her to shut up and stop bothering them, and that little girl simply stood there crying and saying 'I am so sorry, Mommy,' over and over.

"Then her mother sent another barrage of impressively pearly cuss words at the man, he screamed some equally foul things back at her, she flipped him the bird, jumped into the car, and just—okay, I expected her to squeal the tires and burn rubber getting out of there, y'know, make a grand, loud, dramatic, white-trash exit, but she just … drove away, normal speed, like she was going to the grocery store or Bing-Go. The little girl, screaming and crying, ran after the car until she fell over and dropped something, and then she just laid there in that filthy fucking parking lot near the over-loaded Dumpsters, choking on her tears and shouting, 'Please, Mommy, come back, come back, I promise I will be better,' until her voice was completely gone. No one, including me—I'm ashamed to admit—came outside to see if they could help her. The man who must have been her father slammed the door to the apartment and ... *left* her outside. It was thirty-five goddamn degrees, and she wasn't wearing any coat or even slippers. The poor thing was dressed only in pajamas.

"I can't stop thinking that, right then, laying out there all alone like she was, I can't stop thinking that that little girl died. Not physically, but I think a large part of if not all of her childhood bought the farm right there and then. I can't help thinking that some kinda ... kinda *hole* opened in her, maybe—shit, *probably*—the first of its kind. And there's gonna be so many more like it to break her until she shatters like a porcelain statue dropped on a stone-tiled floor. Maybe things'll get better and there'll come a time when she's laughing at ... I dunno ... at a parking-lot carnival again, enjoying the rides and cotton candy and hot dogs and carousels ... but she won't ever again enjoy them as much, because a part of her will always, always remember the way her mother and father treated her like an annoying stray dog in the middle of the night when she tried to express her deepest feelings and found, like, y'know, like any child that age would, that she didn't have the vocabulary to articulate the emotions that no kid her age should *have to be forced* into expressing. She'll have fun at these parking-lot carnivals, but it won't be the same, not ever, not really, not again. Every moment of joy she experiences from now on will be ... *tainted* by the memory of that night, by the hurtful hole it left in her heart and spirit.

"I wanted to kill both of her parents that night. I did eventually drag myself up and managed to roll out to see if I could help, but by then her father had come out and climbed on his shiny, well-cared-for Harley hog and tore out of there like dear old John Wayne himself and the boys were charging right up his ass. And that little girl, she just ... just sat there. She couldn't even cry anymore. She looked so far past lonely ... she looked ... *sick*. I don't mean like the flu or the measles or anything like that ... no. This was the kind of sick you feel when you see some poor dog or cat that's been run over, its insides and fur spread out like some gory blanket, and you feel terrible because somewhere in your head you're wondering that maybe you could have been able to save it *if only*—even though you know that's impossible because what's done is dead, but you hold onto that 'if only' scenario because it makes it easier to pretend that you've succeeded in … in *un*-seeing a thing that terrible. The kind of self-deceiving sick that you know you're going to have to master if you want to keep the impending holes at bay for as long as possible.

"That's the kind of sick I saw in her four-or-five-year-old face.

"Who was it that insisted children are so resilient? Personally, I think that the person who came up with that dose of happy horseshit did so in order to clear their conscience, so they wouldn't have to take any goddamn responsibility for the irreparable damage too many parents do to their children, the little cruelties, the unthinking hurts that get inflicted on a daily basis.

"I feel like I'm rambling. If I were a more concise man, a more eloquent man, and this were a note, it'd be brief and to the point, something like, *I've tried, I really have, but it's not getting better, it's getting worse, and the loneliness is now something I've grown used to, my companion, my friend. And I hate it.*

"I really wanted to kill that little girl's parents. Because they made me finally understand what I'd been fighting for all that time In Country. I was fighting for the freedom of everyone in our noble society to feel justified in tainting everyone and everything around them, the freedom to blast holes and choke the joy out of life and wallow in the squalor which they wrought and not even feel bad about it, even as that corrupted porcelain doll drops to the stone floor and shatters.

"I hope that little girl didn't catch something like pneumonia. She sat out there for a good half-hour, forty-five minutes before her mom came back. *Jeez-us* was that woman pissed that dear old Dad just left the girl out there. She scooped her up and hugged her and carried her back inside—and you here's the part that proves God is probably a sadist and doesn't even know it—the fucking door was *unlocked the whole time!*

"My dad was a soldier in WW2 and knew all about killing people he didn't know. I don't know that he ever got a decent night's sleep because of the memories of the war, everything he saw, all the people he killed. Any of this sound familiar, guys?" He tapped the letter against his remaining leg.

"He used to tell me about something his mother would say to him when he was a child. Whenever he would get sad or heartbroken or lonely, she would stroke his hair and tell him, 'Don't cry, honey, because if you outgrow a certain kind of happiness, or if it gets taken from you, it passes on to someone else who needs it more.' He tried to take comfort in that thought, always tried to make sure I'd grow up to be a good son, but I ...

"I always thought I was a good person, a person who always tried to do the right thing, who did his best to not bring any pain or sorrow into this world—well, after he got back home, anyway—and I always figured that on the day of my death I would be remembered as a decent-enough human being.

"But a decent human being, a *truly* decent human being, would have gone right out into that parking lot as soon as the car pulled away and taken that sad little girl into his arms and stroked her hair and said, 'Don't cry honey, because if you outgrow a certain kind of happiness, or if it gets taken from you, it passes on blah-blah-blah, cha-cha-cha, and so forth.' As if it hangs around forever like some panhandler outside the bus station on a Friday night.

"But it doesn't stick around, does it? It crumbles into dust and is forgotten and any meaning it ever had is shown to be a lie. Watching that little girl sitting so alone in the parking lot made me understand that, and in a strange kind of way, I am thankful, 'cause I realized there's a particular kind of emptiness that only those near the end of ... of something ... something like reason, or maybe rationalization is the better word—y'know, 'I stick around because I want to see the next *Star Wars*' movie or some such horseshit—anyway, there's a certain kind of emptiness that you can only feel and truly understand if you realize you've outlived your purpose. Assuming you had one in the first place.

"No smartass remarks," he said to the wall. "Not one wisecrack, if you please."

The wall was respectfully silent.

"Hey, do you guys like movies? There have been a lot of good ones that you maybe saw ... in whatever kind of movie theater they have where you are. I've gotten pretty decent at imitating some famous scenes. I do a damn good Jack Nicholson—*'You can't handle the truth!'* Or there's my Roy Scheider, *'You're Gonna need a bigger boat.'* I'll spare you my Brando in *The Godfather* routine; I'm still polishing that one. But I got one here that's a real show-stopper." He lifted the pistol, pressing the business end against his temple. "And now, for my next and last and greatest imitation—Christopher Walken in *The Deer Hunter.*"

His breath caught between his lungs and throat when he saw his reflection. This wasn't right. It would be an insult to do this here, it would be like pissing on the memories of these men whose faces he now clearly saw reflected back at him from behind the freeze-frame shot—but were these the opening credits or the closing ones? He felt his grip weaken and lowered the pistol before he dropped it and accidentally shot himself in the nuts. He placed the weapon back in his coat pocket and pulled away his shaking hand.

"I wish to hell I was there with all of you," he said. "I wish I was anywhere but here. I can't … I don't know how I can explain it but … *everything* hurts; my body constantly hurts outside, my thoughts hurt inside my head—and I *know* how pitiful that sounds, but I can't figure how else to express it to you guys, how to explain what I'm gonna do … everything hurts *even when it doesn't*, if you can make sense out of that. I don't even care if there's a Heaven or Hell or weird scenes inside the gold mine."

The dozens of faces reflected from within the wall stared impassively.

He leaned forward, pressing the palm of his hand against the warm black granite, lowering his head and staring at the empty space where his leg used to be. "Do you suppose there's such a thing as an amputated soul, guys? Because that's what it's felt like for the last forty years." He closed his eyes and released a heavy, ragged, staccato breath. "I miss … everyone. Everything. I haven't been able to get back on track since coming home and goddammit *I've tried*, tried my saggy old-man's ass off. I keep waking up every day hoping that the guy I used to be will show back up, and then I wonder if maybe he *did* and I was in the shower and didn't hear the doorbell.

"What the hell am I supposed to do?"

He looked up at his reflection and saw at once there was something different about it. He wasn't wearing his boonie hat, for one thing, even though he could still feel it on his head. His hair seemed fuller. And he was laughing. The reflected faces of the soldiers were no longer impassive; they looked insane, blood-crazed, if they'd been let in on some Big Dark Secret. The man in the wheelchair watched as his hand began to melt into the wall, could feel hands on the other side, hands slick with something warm, grab him by the wrist and yank forward, wrenching him from the wheelchair, and now he was on his one knee, his head thrown back as he struggled to pull himself free, but the more he struggled the less there was of him to struggle with; he felt his muscles tearing, heard the strained popping of tendons and the crackle of bones about to snap. A great pressure began to collapse his body from within. His left hip cracked, liquified, and was gone, as well as part of his back, and the pressure of his broken and crossed right leg against his stomach was almost too much to bear. He opened his mouth to scream but what came out along was a ragged, clogged, wet, pitiful gagging bleat of helplessness; he tried again to scream, to maybe yes maybe *pleasegod* get the attention of someone, anyone, even the night people, the drunks and the prostitutes and kids out to get high, but as he tried to do it there was, at last, no sound; it wouldn't have mattered even if there been. There was no one to hear it. The wheelchair was empty. There was no one there to see the face of the man who once sat in it; the inverse reflection from within the wall was that of a man screaming, constantly screaming, perpetually screaming, a scream that would never stop.

÷

THE next morning when employees of the Cedar Hill O-Hi-O Parks and Recreation Department arrived to gather the tributes left along the wall the previous day—most of which had dried from the rain or were nearly dry—they were shocked to find an abandoned wheelchair parked almost right against the surface of the last section. Propped up on the wheelchair's seat was an envelope that had seen better days, from the looks of it, addressed with childlike handwriting. It would remain unopened, keeping forever the secrets of its content.

*Dear Dad:*

*I'm still here on the bridge but we're leaving tomorrow.*

*A group of volunteers from my platoon went out on a routine patrol this morning and came across a 155-mm artillery round that was booby-trapped. It killed three men, blew the legs off another, and injured two more.*

*And it all turned out a bad day made even worse. On their way back to camp, they saw a woman working in the fields. They shot and wounded her. Then they kicked her almost to death and then emptied their magazines into her head. After that, they beat every kid they came across and killed at least one of them.*

*Why in God's name does this have to happen? I mean, these are seemingly normal guys; some of them were friends of mine. But for a while they became wild animals. Some of them still were like that; angry, frenzied, violent, bloodthirsty. Maybe it's because this is a war without any front lines, against an enemy that might as well be invisible, or could be any person you see—guerrillas waiting in ambush in the jungle or old ladies and children—people we think of as "friendlies"—only they've been trained to set booby traps that blow men apart in their bodies, hearts, and minds.*

*I'm not making excuses for what they did. It was murder, and I'm ashamed of myself for not doing anything about it. I could have gone with them but I didn't. They all just went crazy. Most of them have even tried putting blame on me, like. If only you'd been with us, maybe you could have talked sense, calmed the others down, implored them to show mercy or something.*

Deserving of it or not, I think I'm going to have to carry that shame until the day I die.

And this isn't the first time, Dad. I've seen it many times before. I don't know why I'm telling you all this. I guess I just wanted to get it off my chest, out of my system, so maybe I can convince myself not to feel guilty and think the whole damn world's coming apart at the seams.

My faith in my fellow man is shot to hell, and I'm scared it's going to stay that way. I just want the time to pass so I can come home in something besides a box or a bag.

Tomorrow we're going to be dropped by air near a suspected N.V.A. stronghold. I can't tell you its name because we haven't been told yet. One of those bullshit "Need To Know" things. So I guess that means they tell us once we're airborne.

I love and miss you and Mom so much —

Your Son,

____

# LAIRD BARON

## VERSUS VERSUS

÷

IT was an ominously cool midsummer's evening in the heart of the Catskills at the Hunsucker residence. My "children," Stein and Gertrude, traded barbs near the smoldering hearth of our rustic home. The house, fondly dubbed Satan's Den by dearly departed "Great Aunt" Amrutha, predated electricity and modern plumbing; constructed of timbers, planks, stone slabs, and dirt. Holes in the warped floorboards revealed the glint of a sluggish creek meandering through the cellar. Caverns delved below the foundation; giant vampire bats colonized the attic. All the amenities, you might say. As far as the (secret) records were concerned, the boggy estate suffered an ancient curse or haunting, or both. Nothing but miles of forest tenanted by hoot owls. Creepy and isolated, especially at night, if you were into that sort of thing.

"Memory derives from a prehistoric virus." Stein lit a Gauloises, the venerable brand favored by effete painters and philosophers. "After eons of evolution, the mechanism remains erratic, difficult to quantify, and notoriously fickle."

Gertrude removed her yellow headphones and slid them around her neck. Faint strains of Electric Six played on. "Original thesis or did you steal it?" She made a curving motion with her hands. "Say from the oracle of oracles, the crystal ball of the Zoomer era, Charles Fort's digital age refuge?"

"Yes, yes, it was an internet article. Solid university references, nonetheless. The premise seems sound."

"Sound as a rotten gourd."

"Scoff as you wish, my D-average friend. I'll soon test the theory."

"On whom?" she said. "The peasants are already restless. They've noticed a shitload of disappearances over the winter. Even the bumpkin cops will connect the dots eventually."

"For the love of the Dark, don't give them undue credit, Sis." Stein smoothed his goatee in a sign of high agitation. "An artist creates an object; patrons uncritically appreciate the endeavor. Then some twat comes along. In any event, I shall conjure the Crimson Dream Mist and thus indemnify myself against exposure by the dubious analytical faculties of the sheriff's department."

The "kids" presented as youngish teens—albeit, Stein sported a curiously mature mustache and goatee, and Gertrude unnerved folks with her wickedly pointy smile, raven-wing hairdo, and thousand-yard stare. A goth girl, although more Visi- in the sense of sharing kinship with the tribes who sacked the living shit out of Rome. Stein, versed in the blackest arts, had lately mastered three of the *Nocturnal Grimoires, Jenkins' Field Guide to Supernatural Terror*, and painstakingly revised *Funk & Wanger's Lexicon of Dread*. Each of these tomes of quaint and curious lore eluded even my own semi-formidable intellect, so I was a proud "papa." A relative underachiever and inveterately contrary, Getrude nonetheless defied physics in unique ways to facilitate her murderous hobbies, proving that one can't teach genius. You wouldn't want to meet either of them in a dark alley. This went double for my "wife" Erinyes, the enforcer of the "family," and Stalker and Sid, our "dog" and "cat." Who knew where any of these latter worthies might be at that moment? Although were I to hazard a guess, I'd guess committing acts of terror. Meanwhile, I read the paper and kept half an eye on the tube TV as it played the local evening news in grainy color. Murder, mayhem, and corporate greed running unchecked. As a long-lost rival of mine was wont to remark, the decline of civilization continued apace. I immodestly liked to think we Hunsuckers were playing our part.

The black rotary jangled like a strangled crow. I picked up on the third ring because that was the rule. The operator asked if I'd accept a collect call. I agreed. Several clicks and deep-sea groans followed. A distorted voice on the other end said, *Mr. Hunsucker, do you love your … family?*

"Is this a trick question?"

*Indeed not, Mr. Hunsucker.*

"There can be no allegiance but allegiance to the Dark."

*Praise the mold and the dark. Praise the Slithering Presences. I hereby challenge your right of continued existence.*

"For whom do you speak? On whose behalf do you lay challenge? The Gray Eminence? The Servitors of the Undulant Ones? A nameless demon of the Fugue?"

*None of the above. In our demesne, material reality flattens like a razor. The voice paused to draw an exultant breath. With acute interest, we have long observed your activities, moiling and scrabbling in the fecund dirt of this planet. Some are satisfied to continue observing. Others favor direct intervention. There remains a distinct lack of consensus. Into this vacuum I leap, an aroused tarantula.*

Well, that certainly painted a picture.

*Brother, it's time to dance. The profane Megaliths from the Dawn of Time. Two-fifty-nine AM. Bring your choice of weapons. Praise Entropy!*

I hung up. The clock read a quarter to seven. Dim already; full sunset in under two hours. "Yeah, praise Entropy. Praise malevolence. Praise the Undulant Gods, each and every one." Not sure how much I meant it.

$$\div$$

THE "kids" retired around eleven with no fatal injuries dealt. I stoked the fire and fetched my favorite knives—a flinty Neolithic dagger recovered from an archaeological dig in the 1950s; the other a World War II bayonet only a cubist, or a cultist, could love. Its point had pierced the livers of Axis and Allied troops alike. I was sharpening them when my lovely E walked in flanked by Stalker and Sid. "Dog" threw himself down at my feet—muddy and stinking. "Cat" sneered and disappeared into the kitchen. "Wife" sat opposite me. She was rosy from the hunt, her long hair wild. Blood stained her jacket. Radiant as a hell queen.

"Someone called." E's teeth were serrated because she was in a mood.

"How did you know?"

"Ozone stench."

"Be serious."

"The lines etched deeply around the corners of your mouth. Fake plastic smile is faker than usual."

"Correct, my love. A special someone called."

Her expression darkened—the moon dimming behind a cloud. "Collect?" She studied me with intensity. "Sweet fuck, I'm right."

"Collect."

"Did this caller X out "Aunt" Amrutha? Have *they* found us?"

"No, not *them*. We can only wish it were that simple. The call originated from much farther afield."

"Long distance."

"Long, long distance. Across the viscid barrier of temporal reality. Beamed from the pulsating galaxy of Fugue Lights. And farther. Definitely farther."

"Whoa," she said. "It's a decade early for an audit."

A fair observation. We'd only inherited "Aunt" Amrutha's ancestral lands the previous year and duly insinuated ourselves within the community. Despite numerous early successes, our best work generally proceeded in its own sweet time, spanning months, often years, before bearing poisonous fruit.

I spat on the whetstone. "My presence is requested at the cromlech at the Hour of the Weasel."

"Damnation, talking to you is like pulling crocodile teeth—so, it's a challenge! They wish to usurp your role as head of the family."

"Honey, honey. I suspect the objective is to absorb my vital essences and grow ever larger, ever stronger. Big fish eats little fish. Same as it ever was."

"Single combat, then."

"Single combat."

"When's the last time you fought a duel? Have you *ever* fought a duel?" E made a claw of her hand. Her nails were thick and lusterless as certain kinds of metal. I was no slouch when it came to brutality. My "wife" *excelled* at violence. Thunder and fury were essentially her reasons for being. "Let me go in your stead. More my cup of tea, yeah? Bonus points: I'm in practice."

"You weren't invited, dear. If I don't come back—"

"Take Stalker." She crossed her arms, thwarted but never defeated. The "dog's" ears twitched. His bloodshot eye opened.

"Fine. If Stalker and I don't return by dawn, burn this place down and scatter yourselves on the Four Winds."

"I'd prefer battle. Go out blazing like a terror star."

"Can't fight city hall. Be smart instead of bellicose. For once, sweetie. Grant a dying fellow his last wish."

She leaned over and took my cold hand in hers. "Last wishes? A bit late for those."

÷

THERE was a detour to hit before marching off to meet my fate at the Megaliths from the Dawn of Time. Even though matters appeared terminally calamitous, protocol needs must be observed. I ascended the creaky treacherous stairs past the second floor which contained the sleeping quarters of our happy "family," and up a much narrower, even more treacherous flight. None tread there except for me on pain of, well, various pains. A wooden panel door, chipped and scratched, guarded the landing. The door couldn't always be trusted as it led to various hostile locales depending on the alignment of the constellations, but tonight it opened to the attic. Here lay a vault of termite-raddled beams, deformed statuary (profiles chiseled into aspects of horror), and cobwebbed piles of debris half-revealed in the feeble shine of my flashlight. Reeked of mildewy death, appropriately.

Lair of Dreadwing, his most invidious marauder of the Borscht Belt, descendant of Ennis Shriek, the original razor-toothed night flyer, peasant defiler. Dreadwing was the primeval, malevolent nemesis of everything that crawled or walked or flew in the region over the past millennia. His cohort clung in furry bunches to the beams—chittering their arousal at the scent of my blood, such as it was; thicker than caramelized motor oil. With earnest trepidation I passed beneath the cauldron and stood before their lord. Dreadwing hung reversed, his beady crimson eyes even with my own. Those eyes had gazed upon blanching native shamans and shrieking Dutch colonists back when roads were deer trails. Gut-ripping talons, throat-puncturing fangs; leathern wings that could've tenderly enfolded me as he ravaged and drank.

I performed requisite gestures of obeisance. "Greetings, scion of Shriek. I'm glad to catch you at rest, fattened as a tick, rather than on the wing."

"Hullo, black blood." His voice was so thin only dogs and certain other creatures could discern its pitch. His lisp tickled my inner ear. "You stink differently this evening."

"You're as perceptive as my wife. I face potential doom. My adrenaline flows, no doubt."

"The beats of your heart are measured, lub-a-dub. You remain tepid. Hard to believe your odor is the odor of fear."

I said, "Those senses of yours are keen although not infallible. My peril is severe."

"The crone who dwelt in this den for a century often remarked the same," he said. "She attracted myriad hazards, beseeching my aid on occasion. *O mighty Dreadwing! O dark master! Mine enemies converge! Help me!* Naturally, I demurred, yet she managed to survive. Cunning bitch. My kind are reclusive, preferring to avoid danger. The so-called perils encroaching upon the Hunsuckers are theirs alone. *Yours* alone."

"No argument, lord," I said. "We court disaster at every turn. Nature of the task. Sooner or later, we'll eat our just desserts. I've received a challenge. The one who awaits me at the Megaliths of Dawn is an avatar of the Beyond, a lurker in the Great Dark. It has swum across the gelid barrier of antilife to penetrate this cosm."

The bat shifted. His weight caused the beam to squeal in protest. "As an agent of chaos, do you not seek to erode the bonds of civilization, to see the works of men ground to a fine powder?"

"Quite. The world is drowning, burning, and eating itself alive. On schedule."

"What, pray tell, am I supposed to gift the man who wants for nothing?"

"The prophecies are writ in the holy claret of saints. They predict that my reckoning is a certainty. I simply wish to defer the appointment. Try to comprehend the gravity of a visit by an avatar. Its goal is to test my mettle, to devour it, like as not. This is the way of the universe. Should I succumb, ripples of destruction might well engulf this house and these lands. Your own colony will doubtless share our fate."

Dreadwing said, "Are you certain your enemy would not reward me for taking his, or *its*, side in the dispute? I can be quite ingratiating."

"Summary death is the sole reward you may expect. The avatar will then fuck off back to the outer dark humming a show tune."

"Hang together or hang separately," the bat lord said, perhaps ironically.

"Good enough for the founding fathers, good enough for thee, I hope. My appeal is one of mutual aid and succor."

Dreadwing sighed, a teakettle venting steam. "Say no more, pallid one. A benefit of venerability is the knowledge of secrets. I will reveal to thee a hidden cache wherein resides an artifact of immense power—a fragment of the Black Kaleidoscope reforged into a weapon. Effective against beings from this plane of exis-tence, particularly devastating versus extra-dimensional interlopers. Belonged to an intrepid Star Conqueror who visited the Earth an eon ago. He made planetfall near this very spot. Wounded, disoriented, vulnerable. My children were thirsty. Bad luck for the traveler."

"His K fragment didn't make much difference," I said.

"The star-farer wasn't afforded the opportunity to defend himself. My human slaves buried his parts separately and scattered the malign implements that were upon his person. I drained them afterward to ensure secrecy. The crone was cognizant of the K frag-ment, but not its location. I resisted her cozening and imprecations. Beware! Though potent, the artifact extracts a toll. You shall have a single chance, assuming the object yet possesses its glamor after so many ages gathering rust."

"Only a single chance?" I said.

"To traffic with the Black Kaleidoscope is to trifle with godly might," he said. "Absent proximity to its original source, the fragment draws upon its wielder's essence. Your soul is a flicker compared to the inferno of a Star Blooded. You will undoubtedly be snuffed like a birthday candle."

"I rather enjoyed the prospect of blasting the entity with this weapon until you got to the part where there's a catch—"

"There's always a catch. Sacrificing your puny existence to thwart an avatar of cosmic evil is a fair trade in the greater scheme, wouldn't you agree?"

No, not really. I thanked him anyway and inquired as to the coordinates of this wondrous device.

"Twenty human paces south of the derelict well. Mark a dead cottonwood the crone and her brood called the Hanging Tree. What you seek is buried in its roots. Go, tepid one. Go and have a pleasant death struggle." Dreadwing covered his face, dismissing me.

I departed as swiftly as seemed dignified. The clan fluttered and muttered restless disapproval at permitting succulent prey to escape. Leave well enough alone, lads. You wouldn't have enjoyed the taste of me anyway.

÷

I spun the combination of the steel Diebold safe in the den. The Hunsucker armory. Leather, Hoppe's No. 9, and a melody of dried sweat and adrenaline, wafted forth. Selecting among fanciful costumes and arcane weaponry, I donned finned gauntlets and spiky boots—Dethgrips and steel-toe Face Trampers. These legendary articles were worn by erstwhile champions, every last one of them dead in glorious battle, every one of them dust. I wrapped myself in a scaly black-feathered cloak pinned by a copper clasp of howling Imdugud. From my neck depended a crystalline repelling charm dug out of a chasm near the center of the earth. The knives went into my belt.

Armed and armored, I strolled out across the yard and whistled for Stalker who materialized at my heel like a revenant; drooling, red-glared, trembling with the onset of frenzy. His long, angular profile cast a dozen jangling shadows of the war hounds he'd incarnated as down through the years. Man's best friend. Mine too. We shared a molecular bond of semi-eternal recurrence and unholy blood. Long-lived, but pain was keenly felt.

Dreadwing had told me true—a decayed coffer bound in rusty iron bands lay nestled beneath the roots of "Aunt" Amrutha's Hanging Tree. Similar treasures can be found in many occulted nooks and crannies; you just need a hint. I snapped the brittle lock, removed the artifact (light as a popgun flintlock and faintly cold), and tucked it against the small of my back as a measure of last resort. The chill of the artifact's not-metal seeped into my spine.

Loyal "hound" and I proceeded through the forest. Once, I paused to watch a cacophony of bats boil into the night sky and flap the opposite direction posthaste. No fool, Dreadwing; he'd decided to remove his cauldron from the vicinity. We prowled onward to the cromlech. Its primeval henges were arrayed atop a desolate drumlin rise; a giant's jagged teeth dinged and worn by grinding epochs. The full moon showed its leering visage as I mounted mossy flagstone steps carved into the hillside. Rivers of sacrificial blood had been let at this foul site.

I hesitated at a gap in the prehistoric fangs and recited thusly: "Praise be the punishing gods. Their interlocutors and savants. Praise the chaff that fills the boots of the supreme powers and cushions their soles." I intoned additional supplicatory bullshit as well, in case any adjacent malevolent deities happened to be listening, but that was the gist.

The thick air tasted of burning wire. Dead grass and tarry dirt padded the inner circumference of the cromlech. Wormy earth trod flat by cultists who sailed from dark aged Scandinavia and points south to Burroughs' filthy continent on longboats and astride snarling thunderheads. As the poet said, these villains didn't bring evil with them; the foulness was already here, licking its chops.

Something else waited for me here and now. A shadow materialized at the center of the cromlech. Boiled upward, gaining volume. Taller than the henges; amorphous, and dense as a black hole—blacker—except for pinprick eyes of bubbling magma. The figure cycled through formless forms, each manifesting alien insectile pincers at the end of sucker tentacles. Its central column gave the muzzy impression of a multitude of agape maws; roiling and changeable as Satan's mood ring. It emitted a throbbing static hum.

*Mr. Hunsucker. I've traveled far to greet you.* Its muffled voice popped and stuttered as if still projecting across the bad interstellar connection on my phone. Waves of semi-visible dark energy coruscated outward.

Every hair on my body prickled in response to this mystical irradiation. Stalker pressed his belly to the grass, fangs bared, slobbering mad. His muscles were taut as braided steel cords. He, too, gained density, amplifying his inner "wolf," and would soon become ungovernable, berserk with a rabies of the spirit. As liable to rend me limb from limb as attack our mutual foe.

"Easy, boy." I patted the "dog's" head, forestalling our likely destruction a few more heartbeats. And to the entity, I said, "What purpose does your challenge serve?"

*Again, you've attracted notice.*

"Seldom positive to attract … notice. Our work here is progressing nicely—"

*Indeed, a cell of worker bees, the Hunsuckers, toiling for the dissolution of light and order. And you the master drone. The wilderness of night creeps ever nearer thanks to your unflagging efforts. We certainly approve.*

"It confounds me as to why you initiate conflict," I said. "Seems a waste to interfere …"

*Your goals on this speck of dirt are subordinate to my whims. I acquire the essence of that which interests me. You are interesting. Your family is interesting.*

I drew my blades. Puny as tinfoil. "Conflict it is."

The avatar whirled like a centrifuge. The earth beneath it cracked and sank. Writhing tentacles proliferated. *Your wife usually handles the violence, I hear. Have you lost the taste for it, brother?*

"We shall see."

÷

PUNCH a raging river.

Piss on a forest fire.

Wrestle a tornado.

Shout your fury into a black hole.

Feel your bones bend and snap.

Feel your skin peel away.

Feel your animating force siphoned by a god's drinking straw.

Hear your good and only true friend in the galaxy snarl, then howl, then yelp like a kicked "puppy" as your vision narrows and spinning stars collapse to a pinhole.

Fail.

Beckett levels of failure.

÷

ONCE, in a more romantic era, a Swiss mercenary rammed a can opener pike through my breastplate. Shish-kabobbed me right out of the saddle. On another memorable occasion, a Norman disassembled me with a bearded axe. In more recent times, a German strosstrüppen cooked me and a squad of Army comrades with a jet from his trusty flammenwerfer as we tried to clamber out of a trench. A biker gang stomped me in a deserted parking lot; shot me fourteen times, and pissed on the presumed corpse for good measure. As usual, I returned to testify.

Days gone by, I've had body parts mashed, shorn, and fricasseed by broadswords, speeding tanks, and claymore mines. Been stung, frozen, and chewed up. It's a rough and tumble world, friends. There are a thousand ways to die in this naked galaxy.

So, no, this wasn't the worst thrashing I'd ever received—top five, maybe. Versus had shown restraint. A light maiming, if you will. I crawled toward the house. Left a snail trail of gore shining in the sunrise. My cloak was tattered, my armor shredded. The mystical repelling amulet was blackened as a coal, its chain soldered into my neck. I'd lost the flint knife; the bayonet was slagged to the hilt. My right eye didn't work because it was sort of hanging out of its socket.

E carried me inside, and set me on the couch. Pulled off my smoldering gauntlets and boots. Took the artifact from my waistband and gingerly set it on the coffee table as if handling a holy relic. She applied tourniquets, cradled my head and poured bourbon down my throat. The good stuff we saved for special occasions. Burning hell, better. My astral self, halfway to wherever, began to reel back into my body.

Stein recovered the "dog's" mangled corpse, stuck it in a special birch basket reserved for such dire occasions. He'd been given to me in the exact same basket as a whining and growling "pup." I lay helplessly bleeding as the undying wizard bore Stalker (eyes blinking mute misery) away to his laboratory in the cellar. Could a "boy's" necromantic arts patch Humpty Dumpty together? Improbable, considering the mess of ground meat and viscera slopping around like a pail of chum. Then again, I'd seen stranger things.

Gertrude, a shade paler than usual, adjusted her earphones. Ignoring the hubbub, Sid crouched atop a bookshelf, licking his murder paws in a desultory manner.

E said, "You visited the attic before you went to get killed." She brushed cobwebs from my hair.

"Emergency diplomacy failed," I said, every tooth loose. "Dreadwing declined to help directly."

"No shit. I got the hint when his entire cauldron shook the house, taking flight at one a.m."

"Fancy toy you have here." Gertrude collected herself and perched on the couch armrest. She blithely waved the K fragment. "What kind of artifact is this? Radiates pow-ah …"

Depending on how one squinted, the artifact shimmered like a mirage and transmogrified into a dirk, a club, a sword, or in my estimate, an antique ray gun.

"Take care." I looked her in the eye.

Gertrude's insolent affect didn't extend to foolhardiness. She primly set the item down and yelled for her "brother" who soon appeared, scowling at the interruption—until he saw what had drawn her attention.

"Is that what I think it is?" Stein said. "Where on earth …?"

I said, "Technically, nowhere on earth. This damned curio hails from somewhere so far into the future it's our past. Ancient aliens called it, will call it, a Kaleidoscopic blade. K blade."

"Blade of the Star Conquerors," Stein said.

"Tooth of a wyrm," E said reverently. "Corroded green death."

"A nictitating talisman," Gertrude said. "Shiny!"

"Resembles a wand to me," Stein said. "Resonates at a psychic frequency of mind-altering capability. However, the device's method of operation remains constant, appearances notwithstanding. Something odd, though ..."

"It slices, it dices," I said quickly. "It disintegrates and enervates."

"Why the hell didn't you *disintegrate* the demon outsider?" E said.

"Thought I'd save it for later; lull our foe into a false sense of security. An ace up the sleeve ..."

"You're lucky to have a sleeve. Or an arm."

Truer than she knew.

I held forth my glass for a refill. "Gather round, friends, countrymen. The news isn't good." Recovered enough to guzzle the whole draught and suffer the sweet burn. Hunsucker regenerative qualities are legendary. Add a dose of high-octane blood or one hundred proof booze to the equation, our wounds will practically seal in real time. I went on, "The avatar spared me so that I might contemplate a sinful life and die in the company of my "family." Fairly confident this means whoever remains will share my impending fate."

"Inordinately cruel, even considering the nature of our adversary." Stein stroked his goatee.

I said, "This one's a real bastard. I highly recommend you all depart to greener pastures before dark."

E sneered and folded her arms. A suicidal last stand was precisely her jam. Nor was I in any condition to enforce a command to retreat.

Getrude scooped Sid off his bookshelf perch and fled. "Bully for you, "Mom,"" she called over her shoulder. "I'm Audi 5000."

Who could blame her? My "daughter's" role encompassed reconnaissance, surveillance, and disinformation. Going toe-to-toe with grand eldritch horrors wasn't in the job description.

Stein, wisest of us all, was already gone.

÷

AS the hour of doom drew nigh, I was able to stumble around under my own power. I could make my right hand into a fist. Blind in the right eye. My left arm dangled. Judging by the dizziness, I remained a quart low.

E swiftly barricaded the main doors. She tore floor planks free and screwed them over the windows with a drill gun. Grabbed entrails and jars of clabbered blood from the fridge and painted warding symbols across various thresholds. The effect was slapdash and unlikely to discourage an errant cloud of swamp gas much less an archfiend from Beyond. Warmed my heart that she followed the protocols with utter aplomb, regardless.

Soon the sun set. She switched on a couple of lamps, but the bulbs flared and dimmed. An ominous hush smothered the house. The wall clock stopped. Bird and frog song stopped in the yard. The two of us sat in the creeping blue gloom, awaiting the end.

E said, "You were afraid to pull the trigger."

"Yes," I said.

"Why?"

"The K fragment is a soul sucker."

"Do you have any soul left to suck?"

"Only one way to know and at the moment of truth I quailed."

"Has anything changed over the past few hours?"

I pushed my slipping eyeball back into its socket. "I've come to terms with the notion that mutual destruction is preferable to the alternative."

A thunderous clamor erupted in the distance and rolled across the forest. Trees thrashed. Wind shook the house. Then, as abruptly, the tumult ceased, followed by another lull of suffocating quiet. Someone knocked on the front door.

"Ding, dong." E's long hair straightened and floated above her shoulders.

I expected the wall to be obliterated and Versus to burst in like the Kool-Aid Man; or the upper level to shear away and reveal our nemesis, a gargantuan silhouette, leering down at us. What actually happened? The planks barring the front door fell and clattered. Versus turned the knob and rolled in as casually as an invited guest popping by for tea. It had assumed a buzzing and humming humanoid form—tall, void-black, and featureless except for those radiant eyes.

*We meet again.*

Before I could respond, Stein stepped from the shadows dressed in his ceremonial cloak of skulls. He performed a complex gesture and barked a phrase in a long dead proto-language. Walls shuddered; windows blew outward. My ears rang. Versus' form lost solidity, although it swiftly reconstituted. And in that moment, Gertrude appeared on the landing to the second story aiming a double barrel shotgun I'd kept in the closet for sentimental reasons. She let our visitor have both barrels. The avatar absorbed all that buckshot without apparent discomfort. Gertrude had staggered under the recoil. She yelped and ran upstairs.

A long, unpleasant pause ensued.

The hiss and crackle of Versus' aura indicated confusion or bemusement. *Why do you resist?* Its arms lengthened to initiate a killing blow. *You're agents of doom, fated to usher in the heat death then shuffle off to oblivion.*

"Yes," E said. "But we prefer to shuffle into the void together and with the fullness of time. Another eon, give or take." She met my gaze. "Honey?"

I raised the K fragment in my shooting hand and squeezed the trigger ... Dead click.

"Well, that settles *that* question," E said, smiling grimly.

"Permit me, "Father."" Stein plucked the ray gun from my fingers, cranked the spring and pointed at the center of the avatar's swirling mass. Tucked his left arm behind his back in the pose of a Renaissance duelist plugging an ace of spades at twenty paces.

The avatar's magma eyes flared. *Intriguing weapon. Our intelligence made no reference to your capabilities as a scientist, master necromancer.*

"Scientist? Nay, I simply possess access to hyper advanced weaponry and a will to destroy. Like thus." My "son" annihilated Versus in a soundless beam of coruscating purple fire. When the weapon discharged, the atmosphere grew dense and the feeble illumination dimmed further. Reality bleached. Where the visitor had stood, a black circle crisped the floorboards; another on the ceiling matched.

"Stein," E said in a tone as close to motherly grief as I'd ever heard her express.

The "boy" dropped the K fragment. He opened his mouth, but it burned with more purple energy that gushed forth and consumed him in an instant. His pale disembodied soul, stretched and distorted, rose within a column of flame. The column snuffed, leaving behind another set of scorched circles.

Houselights brightened. Color restored to the mortal plane. We blinked, waiting and waiting, ready for the other hobnail boot to fall. It didn't. The incident seemed to be over but for the gods damned mess.

÷

NIGHTS grew chilly and long. On one of them, in the Hour of the Bat, I reclined in my chair, wrapped in a blanket and sipping whiskey, Stalker's basket at my feet. The dying fire reminded me of recent horrors.

The phone rang.

*Mr. Hunsucker, I trust you're recovering,* Versus said over the static.

Bleary vision had returned to my eye. My injured arm was more or less attached. Most of the deep lacerations had faded. Beneath the surface, matters were less rosy. A storm boiled in my mind.

"Just swell," I said. "You're less dead than I hoped."

*Avatar is not a figure of speech. My kind don't risk our primary form on hazardous expeditions. You destroyed a projection. Kudos, though.* It waited for a response that was never coming. In a while it said, *Don't be angry, Mr. Hunsucker. This ordeal was an unscheduled audit. Your cell performed adequately and retained operational coherence under extreme duress. You will continue to function in your current capacity. Until we meet anon.* The connection severed.

I swallowed the last of the booze. Thought a thousand useless murderous thoughts.

÷

SEVERAL days later, I stood on the porch, warming Stalker's basket in the bleak late afternoon sunlight. He still couldn't do much in his diminished condition, but I heard him sniffing the breeze off the bog ripe with odors of musk and dead meat.

An adolescent boy walked along the bumpy driveway, suitcases in hand. Pallid, slim, blond. Sharp eyes as blue as a glacier. Dressed in an old-fashioned black suit and polished shoes. He cast a strange, long shadow over the dirt and the withered grass. Birds flew away from him, dashing themselves in the trees and against the clapboard walls of the house.

He set his suitcases down to shake my hand. His clammy grip was impressive.

"My name is Boaz. Boaz Hunsucker." He glanced around, taking in the sights, such as they were. "I'm your "son.""

"Hi, "son." Welcome home."

A muffled high-pitched growl issued from the basket. The lid rattled.

"Who's in there?" the "boy" said.

"Oh, that's Stalker," I said. "He's ... Well, he's recovering."

Boaz smiled. He had plenty of teeth. "Gosh, I've always wanted a dog."

# JAMAL HODGE

## THE THIRD SEAL

÷

WHEN the Euphrates River dried,
4 blaring trumpets, 8 blackened wings.

*"A quart of wheat for a denarius,
and three quarts of barley for a denarius;
but do not damage the oil and the wine."*

The farm animals, first.
Pets soon follow,
when hunger thirsts.

The crops have failed,
the meat long used.
Eyes and teeth wander,
seeking flesh to abuse.

A groaning belly,
makes a strong case to the mind,
finds the steak in a man,
the sirloin in a son.
Chickens,
are females to a one.

Some use grease,
salt and pepper, laid on thick,
a butcher's knife to the esophagus
ends their protests quick.

Foreigners
are first to be deported
down a toilet's maw.
Flushed outside of memory,
bone white, steaming, raw.

Asking moral questions,
disappear, the fattest first.
Melted grizzle of Barbecue,
amending
the feaster's thirst.

Parents consult in secret.
What of the children,
now that they can't be fed?
The population decreased
so suddenly,
the surplus of the dead.

What of the children,
these tender-skins
suffering so? Are they to endure
needlessly, as they shrink
and inevitably go?

Such a waste, to go untasted,
a bag of bones so thin.
Shall a Mother waste
what her body cultivated,
or let the hunger win?

Who among the starving
confuses mercy for abuse?
From the noblest of sacrifices,
comes the noblest of use.

Empty playgrounds tell the story,
pots hide beneath their lids.
A silencing of little feet,
no laughter from the kids.

Parents, in their homes,
hide the renewed color
in their cheeks,
the full roundness of their bellies,
from sustenance it speaks:

*"A quart of wheat for a denarius,*
*and three quarts of barley for a denarius;*
*but do not damage the oil and the wine."*

# THE AUTHORS

**ZOJE STAGE** is the *USA Today* and internationally bestselling author of the psychological thrillers *Baby Teeth*, *Dear Hanna*, and *Getaway*, and the psychological horror novels *Wonderland* and *Mothered*. Her books have been named "best of the year" by Forbes Magazine, Library Journal, PopSugar, LitReactor, Barnes & Noble, Book Riot, and more. She lives in Pittsburgh with her cats.

**ALEX GRECIAN** is the *New York Times* bestselling author of *The Yard* and its sequels *The Black Country*, *The Devil's Workshop*, *The Harvest Man*, and *Lost and Gone Forever*, as well as the contemporary thriller *The Saint of Wolves and Butchers*, and the ebook *The Blue Girl*. He has written multiple award-winning graphic novels, including *Proof* and *Rasputin*.

**CHUCK PALAHNIUK**'s nine novels are the bestselling *Snuff*, *Rant*, *Haunted*, *Lullaby*, and *Fight Club*, which was made into a film by director David Fincher, *Diary*, *Survivor*, *Invisible Monsters*, and *Choke*, which was made into a film by director Clark Gregg. He is also the author of the nonfiction profile of Portland, *Fugitives and Refugees*, and the nonfiction collection *Stranger Than Fiction*. He lives in the Pacific Northwest.

**ANNA TABORSKA** was born in London, England. She studied Experimental Psychology at Oxford University and went on to gainful employment in public relations, journalism, and advertising, before throwing everything over to become a filmmaker and horror writer. Anna has directed two short films (*Ela* and *The Sin*), two documentaries (*My Uprising* and *A Fragment of Being*) and a one-hour television

drama (*The Rain Has Stopped*), which won two awards at the British Film Festival, Los Angeles. She has also worked on seventeen other films, including Ben Hopkins' *Simon Magus* (starring Noah Taylor and Rutger Hauer). Anna worked as a researcher and assistant producer on several BBC television programmes, including *Auschwitz: The Nazis and the Final Solution* and *World War Two: Behind Closed Doors – Stalin, the Nazis and the West*. Anna's feature length screenplays include: *Chainsaw, The Camp, Pizzaman* and *The Bloody Tower*. Short screenplays include: *Little Pig* (finalist in the Shriekfest Film Festival Screenplay Competition), *Curious Melvin*, and *Arthur's Cellar*. Anna's short stories have been reprinted in *The Best New Horror of the Year, Best British Horror, Year's Best Weird Fiction,* and *JWK Fiction Best of Horror*. Anna's short story 'Bagpuss' was an Eric Hoffer Award Honoree and published in *Best New Writing 2011*, and 'Little Pig' from *The Eighth Black Book of Horror* was a runner-up for the Abyss Awards. Her poetry has been published in four anthologies and in the *Journal of Dramatic Theory and Criticism*. Anna's debut collection, *For Those Whoe Dream Monsters*, won the Dracula Society's Children of the Night Award and was nominated for a British Fantasy Award. Her latest collection, *Bloody Britain*, was nominated for a Bram Stoker Award and two British Fantasy Awards.

NGO BINH ANH KHOA is a teacher of English in Ho Chi Minh City, Vietnam. In his free time, he enjoys reading fiction and writing speculative poems and stories, many of which have appeared in *Space and Time Magazine, Star\*Line, Weirdbook, Spectral Realms, NewMyths.com*, as well as other venues and anthologies. He also enjoys writing haiku, some of which have received awards and honorable mentions in international contests in the US, the UK, Japan, Canada, and elsewhere.

CYNTHIA PELAYO is a Bram Stoker Award-winning and International Latino Book Award-winning author and poet. She writes fairy tales that blend genre and explore concepts of grief, mourning, and cycles of violence. She is the author of *Loteria, Santa Muerte, The Missing, Poems of My Night, Into the Forest and All the Way Through, Chil-*

dren of Chicago, Crime Scene, The Shoemaker's Magician, as well as dozens of standalone short stories and poems. *Loteria*, which was her MFA in Writing thesis at The School of the Art Institute of Chicago, was re-released to praise with *Esquire* calling it one of the 'Best Horror Books of 2023.' *Santa Muerte* and *The Missing*, her young adult horror novels, were each nominated for International Latino Book Awards. *Poems of My Night* was nominated for an Elgin Award. *Into the Forest and All the Way Through* was nominated for an Elgin Award and was also nominated for a Bram Stoker Award for Superior Achievement in a Poetry Collection. *Children of Chicago* was nominated for a Bram Stoker Award for Superior Achievement in a Novel and won an International Latino Book Award for Best Mystery. *Crime Scene* won the Bram Stoker Award for Superior Achievement in a Poetry Collection. *The Shoemaker's Magician* has been released to praise with Library Journal awarding it a starred review. Her novel *The Forgotten Sisters* was released by Thomas and Mercer in 2024 and is an adaptation of Hans Christian Andersen's "The Little Mermaid." Her works have been reviewed in *The New York Times*, *Chicago Tribune*, *LA Review of Books*, and more.

**ELIZABETH MASSIE** is the author of numerous novels for young adult, middle grade, and primary readers. These include the *Young Founders* series, the *Daughters of Liberty* trilogy, *The Great Chicago Fire: 1871*, *The Fight for Right*, *Read All About It*, and more. A former middle school teacher, Elizabeth enjoys exploring both important and little-known moments in American history and presenting those moments to readers through the struggles and triumphs of her characters. Elizabeth lives in the historic Shenandoah Valley of Virginia, very close to where her family moved in 1747. She says, "Every place is historic. Well-known or not, every town, city, and county has its own compelling tale of people and events, a story that plays a part in the continuing story that is our history."

**JOHN F.D. TAFF** is a Bram Stoker Award short-listed horror and dark fiction author with more than 25 years experience, and more than

100 short stories and seven novels in print. He has appeared in *Cemetery Dance*, *Eldritch Tales*, *Unnerving*, *Deathrealm*, *Big Pulp*, and *One Buck Horror*. Recent anthology contributions include *The Seven Deadliest* and *I Can Hear the Shadows*. Taff's novella collection, *The End in All Beginnings*, was called one of the best novella collections by Jack Ketchum and was a Stoker Award finalist.

**ANDY DAVIDSON** is the Bram Stoker Award-nominated author of *In the Valley of the Sun*, *The Boatman's Daughter*, and *The Hollow Kind*. His novels have been listed among NPR's Best Books, the New York Public Library's Best Adult Books of the Year, and *Esquire's* Best Horror of the Year. His short stories have appeared online and in print journals, as well as numerous anthologies, most recently the Shirley Jackson Award-winning *The Hideous Book of Hidden Horrors* from Bad Hand Books, and Ellen Datlow's *Best Horror of the Year Volume 15*. Born and raised in Arkansas, Andy makes his home in Georgia, where he teaches creative writing at Middle Georgia State University. He lives with his wife, Crystal, and a bunch of cats.

**MASON IAN BUNDSCHUH** is a writer, musician, and trouble-maker from Kauai, Hawaii. He'll have you know that first. Being from a small, rural, tight-knit island, a place where everyone and everything is forced to slow down, an ethnic and cultural melting pot, a place with old scars but much aloha, has shaped him in a peculiar way. His growing publishing credits in various award-winning anthologies both humbles him and makes him proud. He also once punched a shark.

**JONATHAN LEES** originally hails from a shuttered mill town in New England and can now often be spotted lurking in the alleys of New York or within the barrens of New Jersey. In addition to fifteen years of creating strategies and video series for outlets ranging from Complex Media to TIDAL, he has also spent decades championing independent filmmakers through his work with the New York Under-

ground Film Festival, Anthology Film Archives, and more. He has been writing for as long as he can remember.

LORA SENF is a wife and a mom to twins. She is also a writer of dark and twisty stories for all ages, and the author of the middle grade *Blight Harbor* books, including *The Clackity*, the Bram Stoker Award-winning *The Nighthouse Keeper*, and *The Loneliest Place*. Her debut young adult dark fantasy *The Losting Fountain* is coming December 31, 2024. Lora finds inspiration for her writing in her children's retellings of their dreams, on road trips through Montana, and most recently in an abandoned abattoir and at the Anaconda Smoke Stack. As a young reader, she raised herself on classic fairy tales, John Bellairs, Ray Bradbury, and Stephen King (she read *Cujo* when she was eight and was simultaneously terrified and hooked). Today, she still prefers a rainy day and a scary book to nearly anything else. In her free time, you can generally find her reading a book—mostly horror but anything a little weird and unsettling will do. Lora credits her love of words to her parents and to the public library that was walking distance from her childhood home. Lora is a member of the Horror Writers Association. You can find her spending far too much time on Twitter @Lora013.

AI JIANG is a Chinese-Canadian writer and winner of the Bram Stoker, Nebula, and Ignyte Awards, and a Hugo, Astounding, Locus, and BSFA Award finalist, and an immigrant from Shanghu, Changle, Fujian currently residing in Toronto, Ontario. Find her on most social media platforms, and for more information go to aijiang.ca.

SCOTT EDELMAN has published 125+ short stories in magazines such as *Lightspeed*, *Analog*, *Apex*, and *The Twilight Zone*, and in anthologies such as *Why New Yorkers Smoke*, *Crossroads: Southern Tales of the Fantastic*, and *MetaHorror*. His collection of zombie fiction, *What Will Come After*, was a finalist for the Shirley Jackson Memorial Award, and his science fiction short stories have been collected in *What We Still Talk About*. His most recent collection is *Things That Never Happened*, which caused Publishers Weekly to write, "his talent is undeniable." He has been a Bram Stoker Award finalist eight times.

EUGEN BACON is an African Australian author of several novels and collections. She's a British Fantasy Award winner, a Foreword Indies Award winner, a twice World Fantasy Award finalist, and a finalist in other awards. Eugen was announced in the honor list of the Otherwise Fellowships for 'doing exciting work in gender and speculative fiction.' *Danged Black Thing* made the Otherwise Award Honor List as a 'sharp collection of Afro-Surrealist work,' and was a 2024 Philip K Dick Award nominee. Eugen's creative work has appeared worldwide, including in *Apex Magazine*, and *Award Winning Australian Writing, Fantasy, Fantasy & Science Fiction*, and *Year's Best African Speculative Fiction*. Visit her at eugenbacon.com.

CLAY McLEOD CHAPMAN writes books, comic books, children's books, as well as for film and television. His most recent novels include *Ghost Eaters* and *What Kind of Mother*. You can find him at claymcleodchapman.com.

ERIC LaROCCA (he/they) is a two-time Bram Stoker Award finalist and Splatterpunk Award winner. Named by *Esquire* as one of the "Writers Shaping Horror's Next Golden Age" and praised by *Locus* as "one of the strongest and most unique voices in contemporary horror fiction," LaRocca's notable works include *Things Have Gotten Worse Since We Last Spoke, Everything the Darkness Eats, The Trees Grew Because I Bled There: Collected Stories*, and *You've Lost a Lot of Blood*. His upcoming novel, *At Dark, I Become Loathsome*, will be published in January 2025. The book has already been optioned for film by *The Walking Dead* star Norman Reedus. He currently resides in Boston, MA with his partner.

GARY A. BRAUNBECK is a prolific author who writes mysteries, thrillers, science fiction, fantasy, horror, and mainstream literature. He is the author of 24 books—evenly divided between novels and short story collections; his fiction has been translated into Japanese, French, Italian, Russian, German, Czech, and Polish. Nearly 200 of his stories have appeared in various publications. He was born in Newark, Ohio, the city that serves as the model for the fictitious Cedar Hill in many of his novels and stories, which are collected in *Graveyard People*, *Home Before Dark*, and the forthcoming *The Carnival Within*, all published by Earthling. His fiction has received several awards, including seven Bram Stoker Awards: the first for Superior Achievement in Short Fiction in 2003 for "Duty"; the second—also for Superior Achievement in Short Fiction—in 2005 for "We Now Pause for Station Identification"; his collection *Destinations Unknown* won the Stoker for Superior Achievement in a Fiction Collection in 2006; and 2007 saw Gary winning two Stokers, the first for co-editing the anthology *Five Strokes to Midnight* (nominated for The World Fantasy Award that same year), and the second for his novella *Afterward, There Will Be a Hallway*. In 2011 his book *To Each Their Darkness* received the Stoker for Superior Achievement in Non-Fiction; and in 2013, his novella *The Great Pity* took home the Stoker for Superior Achievement in Long Fiction. His novella *Kiss of the Mudman* received the International Horror Guild Award for Long Fiction in 2005. As an editor, Gary completed the latest installment of the *Masques* anthology series created by Jerry Williamson, *Masques V*, after Jerry became too ill to continue. He also served a term as president of the Horror Writers Association. His nonfiction book *To Each Their Darkness* has been used as a text by several college writing classes, and Gary has taught writing seminars and workshops around the country (including a week-long stint as the Writer in Residence at the 2011 Odyssey Writers Workshop) on topics such as short story writing, characterization, and dialogue. His work is often praised for its depth of emotion and characterization, as well as for its refusal to adhere to any genre tropes; some joke that the term "cross-genre fiction" may have been invented to describe his work—a rumor he does everything in his power to propagate.

LAIRD BARRON, an expat Alaskan, is the author of several books, including *The Imago Sequence and Other Stories*, *Swift to Chase*, and *Blood Standard*. Currently, Barron lives in the Rondout Valley of New York State and is at work on tales about the evil that men do.

JAMAL HODGE is a Native New Yorker who grew up surrounded by the perils of poverty, the diversity of multiple overlapping cultures, and the harmonious circus of six siblings. He is a multi-award-winning film director whose one obsession is exploring the great 'Why?' inside each of us. Jamal loves the broken things that want to be understood, and the secret things that never bothered to hide. With his writing he hopes to uncover the paradox between suffering and meaning, to use darkness to show light. When he's not writing or filming, he is traveling to odd locales, volunteering at some community organization, or in the gym working out to a near-death experience. He fancies himself a pretty cool guy.

# THE EDITORS

DOUG MURANO is the Bram Stoker Award-winning and Shirley Jackson Award-winning founder and chief creative officer of Bad Hand Books. His anthologies include *The Hideous Book of Hidden Horrors*, *Behold! Oddities, Curiosities & Undefinable Wonders*, and *Miscreations: Gods, Monstrosities & Other Horrors* (edited with Michael Bailey). He lives somewhere on the Great Plains with his wife, their four children, and an enormous Labrador Retriever named Alice. Find Bad Hand Books on Twitter, Bluesky, Facebook, Instagram, and at badhandbooks.com.

MICHAEL BAILEY is a recipient and nine-time nominee of the Bram Stoker Award, a five-time Shirley Jackson Award nominee, and a three-time recipient of the Benjamin Franklin Award, along with an insane number of independent accolades through his press Written Backwards. He has written, edited, and published many books, such as *Silent Nightmares: Haunting Stories to Be Told on the Longest Night of the Year* with Chuck Palahniuk. He is also the screenwriter for *Madness and Writers* and a producer for numerous film projects. He lives in Costa Rica, but find him online at nettirw.com, or on social media @nettirw.

# ALSO AVAILABLE

EDITED BY DOUG MURANO

÷

SHADOWS OVER MAIN STREET
*An Anthology of Small-Town Lovecraftian Terror*
*with D. Alexander Ward*
(vol. 1 - 3)

GUTTED
*Beautiful Horror Stories*
*with D. Alexander Ward*

BEHOLD!
*Oddities, Curiousities, and Undefinable Wonders*

MISCREATIONS
*Gods, Monstrosities, and Other Horrors*
*with Michael Bailey*

THE HIDEOUS BOOK OF HIDDEN HORRORS

# ALSO AVAILABLE

EDITED BY MICHAEL BAILEY

÷

PELLUCID LUNACY

CHIRAL MAD
(vol. 1 - 5)

QUALIA NOUS
(vol. 1 - 2)

THE LIBRARY OF THE DEAD

YOU, HUMAN
*An Anthology of Dark Science Fiction*
(vol. 1 - 2)

ADAM'S LADDER
*with Darren Speegle*

PRISMS
*with Darren Speegle*

SILENT NIGHTMARES
*Haunting Stories to be Told on the Longest Night of the Year*
*with Chuck Palahniuk*

Printed in the United States
by Baker & Taylor Publisher Services